Did he know
"I don't think I'
perhaps..."

But a practical woman wouldn't be locked in his arms, her body rejoicing at the hardness of his, her heart pounding so heavily he must feel it.

"Do you feel practical now?" His voice was low and tender.

She closed her eyes, afraid that he'd see just what she was feeling—total surrender, a desperate, wanton abandonment of all the rules she'd lived by until she'd met him.

"No," she admitted.

"So...how do you feel?" And when she didn't answer he laughed softly. "A little wild?"

He punctuated each word with teasing kisses, but she sensed the inner demands driving him, and something fierce flared up to match his hunger.

"Reckless?" he murmured, his mouth poised so close to hers that their breath mingled.

"Yes," she said, knowing that now there would be no going back—knowing and not caring, because there was nothing in the world she wanted as much as learning about Rafiq in the most intimate way of all.

ROBYN DONALD

Greetings! I'm often asked what made me decide to be a writer of romances. Growing up in a family of readers helped; after anxious calls from neighbors driving our dusty country road, my mother tried to persuade me to wait until I got home before I started reading the current library book, but the lure of those pages was always too strong.

Shortly after I started school I started whispering stories in the dark to my two sisters. Although most of those tales bore a remarkable resemblance to whatever book I was immersed in, it was my first experience of the joy of creativity.

Growing up in New Zealand gave me a taste for romantic landscapes and exotic gardens. But it wasn't until I was in my mid-twenties that I read a Harlequin® Presents book and realized that the country I love came alive when populated by strong, tough men and spirited women.

By then I was married and a working mother, but into my busy life I crammed hours of writing; my family have always been hugely supportive, even the various dogs who have slept on my feet and demanded that I take them for walks at inconvenient times. I learned my craft in those busy years, and when I finally plucked up enough courage to send off a manuscript, it was accepted. The only thing I can compare that excitement to is the delight of bearing a child.

Since then it's been a roller-coaster ride of fun and hard work and wonderful letters from fans. I see my readers as intelligent women who insist on accurate backgrounds as well as an intriguing love story, so I spend time researching as well as writing.

INNOCENT MISTRESS, ROYAL WIFE
ROBYN DONALD

~ ROYAL AND RUTHLESS ~

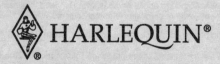

TORONTO • NEW YORK • LONDON
AMSTERDAM • PARIS • SYDNEY • HAMBURG
STOCKHOLM • ATHENS • TOKYO • MILAN • MADRID
PRAGUE • WARSAW • BUDAPEST • AUCKLAND

Recycling programs
for this product may
not exist in your area.

ISBN-13: 978-0-373-52729-8

INNOCENT MISTRESS, ROYAL WIFE

First North American Publication 2009.

Copyright © 2008 by Robyn Donald.

www.eHarlequin.com

Printed in U.S.A.

INNOCENT MISTRESS, ROYAL WIFE

CHAPTER ONE

RAFIQ DE COUTEVEILLE looked directly at Therese Fanchette, the motherly, middle-aged woman whose razor-sharp mind oversaw the security of his island country in the Indian Ocean. In a level voice he asked, 'Exactly what sort of relationship does this Alexa Considine have with Felipe Gastano? Are they lovers?'

Therese said neutrally, 'They are sharing a room at the hotel.'

So they were lovers. Rafiq glanced down at the photograph on his desk. Fine featured, medium height and slim, the woman was laughing up at the man he'd had in his sights for the past two years. She didn't look like Felipe Gastano's sort, but then, he thought with ice-cold anger, neither had Hani. His sister, now dead. 'What have you discovered about her?'

'Not much, but I've just been talking to a source in New Zealand. I taped the conversation, of course, and I'll make a written report after I've had the information verified.' She straightened her spectacles and checked her notes. 'Alexa Considine is twenty-six years old, and in New Zealand she is known as Lexie Sinclair. Until a year ago she was a veterinarian in a rural practice in the north of the country. When her half-sister—Jacoba Sinclair, the model—and Prince Marco of Illyria became engaged, it emerged that Ms Considine is actually the daughter of the dead dictator of Illyria.'

'Paulo Considine?' At her nod, Rafiq's brows lifted. 'How did the daughter of one of the most hated and feared men of the twentieth century grow up in New Zealand?'

'Her mother fled there when the children were very young. She must have had good reason to be terrified of her husband. According to the news media, neither girl had any idea of their real identity until they were adults.'

'Anyone who knew Considine had reason to be afraid. Go on,' Rafiq said, his eyes once more on the photograph.

'She has spent the past year working with the peasants in Illyria, healing their animals and teaching classes at the veterinary college she's helped set up under Prince Alex of Illyria's patronage.' Therese looked up. 'It appears he used her obvious innocence of her father's sins to break the ancient system of blood feuds in his country.'

Yes, Alex of Illyria was clever enough to stage-manage the situation to his advantage, Rafiq thought, his mind racing.

So Felipe Gastano had brought Alexa Considine to Moraze. What the *hell* was her family thinking to allow it? Her cousins were sophisticated men of the world; they must know that Gastano lived on the edge of society, using his wits, his handsome face and the faded glamour of an empty title to dazzle people. The tabloids called Count Felipe Gastano a great lover. Rafiq knew of a woman who'd killed herself after he'd stripped her of her self-respect by seducing her and then introducing her to drugs.

But perhaps Alexa Considine had something of her father in her. In spite of her work for the peasants, she could be an embarrassment to the Illyrian royal family.

Possibly she didn't need protection because she knew very well how to look after herself...

He had to know more before he worked out how best to exploit the situation. 'She and Gastano have been lovers for how long?'

'About two months.'

Rafiq's dark gaze travelled to the handsome face of his enemy. Although he doubted that Gastano felt anything much beyond a cynical, predatory lust for any woman, he had a reputation for pride. He had always demanded beauty in his amours.

But Alexa Considine—Lexie Sinclair—was not beautiful. Attractive, yes, even striking, but without the overt sexuality the man had always favoured. So why had he chosen her to warm his bed?

Brows drawing together, Rafiq studied the photograph of the woman on Gastano's arm. It had been taken at a party in London, and she was laughing up at Gastano's good-looking face.

The illegitimate son of an aristocrat, the man had assumed the title 'Count' after the real count, his half-brother, had died from a drug overdose. Gastano might well consider that the Sinclair woman's connections to the rich and powerful Considine family—tainted though they were—would give him the social standing he'd spent his life seeking.

That certainly made sense. And now Gastano's arrogance and his conviction that he was above suspicion had delivered him into Rafiq's hands.

Transferring his gaze to the crest on the wall of his office, Rafiq reined in a cold anticipation as he surveyed the emblem of his family—a rampant horse wearing a crown that held a glitter of crimson, signifying the precious fire-diamonds found only on Moraze.

Rafiq would not be his father's son—or Hani's brother—if he failed to use the situation to his advantage.

Revenge was an ugly ambition, but Hani's death should not be in vain.

As for Alexa Considine—she might have been innocent before she met Gastano, though it seemed unlikely. Her half-sister had worked in the notoriously amoral world of high fashion, so maybe Alexa Considine had a modern attitude to sex, taking partners as she wanted them.

But if not, he'd be doing her a favour. Felipe Gastano was no considerate lover, and once his world started crumbling around him he'd fight viciously to save himself. She'd be far safer out of the way.

Besides, he thought with cold satisfaction, it would give him great pleasure to take her from Gastano, to show the creep the limits of his power and influence before the trap closed around him.

Mind made up, he said evenly, 'This is what I want you to do.'

Mme Fanchette leaned forward, frowning slightly as he outlined his instructions. When he'd finished she said quietly, 'Very well, then. And the count?'

Rafiq's voice hardened. 'Watch him closely—put your best people onto it, because he's as wary as a cat.' He got up and walked across to the window, looking down at the city spread below. 'Fortunately he is also a man with a huge sense of self-esteem, and a sophisticate's disdain for people who live in small, isolated countries far from the fleshpots of the world he preys on.'

From beneath lowered lashes, Rafiq watched the woman in the flame-coloured dress. Cleverly cut to reveal long legs, narrow waist and high, small breasts, the silk dress angled for male attention. But Alexa Considine's face didn't quite fit its skilful, not entirely discreet sensuality.

The photographs hadn't lied; she wasn't a top-class beauty, Rafiq decided dispassionately—although, like every other woman attending the official opening of Moraze's newest, most luxurious, highly exclusive hotel, she was superbly groomed. Her cosmetics had been applied expertly and her golden-brown hair cut by a master to make the most of her features. However, apart from that eye-catcher of a dress, she stood out, and not just because she was alone.

Gastano, Rafiq noted, was across the other side of the room flirting with a film star of somewhat notorious reputation.

Interesting...

Unlike every other woman in the place, Alexa Considine wore no jewellery. And she looked unawakened, as though no one had ever kissed that tempting, lushly opulent mouth—sensuous enough to make any red-blooded man fantasise about the touch of it on his skin.

Rafiq's gut tightened. Swiftly controlling the hot surge of desire through his blood, he scanned her fine-boned face with an impassive expression. It seemed highly unlikely that her features told anything like the truth. Mme Fanchette's source in New Zealand had come up with a blank about any possible affairs, but that didn't mean

Alexa was an innocent. At university no one would have taken much notice of her love life.

And she was certainly Felipe Gastano's mistress, so that grave, unworldly air had to be spurious, a mere trick of genetics from somewhere in her bloodline.

Yet her cool self-possession challenged Rafiq in some primal, instinctive way. What would it be like to banish the composure from those regular features, set those large, slightly tilted eyes aflame with desire, feel those lips shape themselves to his…?

It took an effort of will to look away and pretend to scan the crowd, carefully chosen for their ability to create a buzz—a gathering wave of gossip and comment that would reach the ears of those who wanted privacy and opulence when they holidayed.

Rafiq had himself vetted the guest list, and apart from the woman in the sunset-coloured dress everybody in this Indian Ocean fantasy of a salon wore their sophistication like a badge of belonging.

Standing alone in the elegant, crowded room, she was attracting interested glances. Rafiq had to rein in a disturbing urge to forge his way through the chattering mob and cut her out, like a stallion with its favourite mare.

As he watched she turned and walked out through the wide doors into the warm, tropical night, the light from the chandeliers gleaming over satiny, golden-amber hair.

Across the room Gastano looked up, said something to the film star, and set off after his mistress. Rafiq fought back a raw anger that drove him to follow Gastano, and moved with the lithe gait of a man in complete control of his body.

He should leave it to the security men, of course, but

he wanted to see them together, Gastano and Alexa Considine. That way he'd know for certain the truth about their relationship.

It was, he thought cynically as he stepped out onto the wide stone terrace, a perfect night for dalliance—the stars were as big as lamps, the sea gleamed like black silk shot with silver, and erotic perfumes from the flower farms of Moraze drifted lazily through the palms.

Stopping in the shadow of a vine heavy with flamboyant scarlet blossom, Rafiq watched the count walk up to Alexa Considine, and fought a primitive impulse to follow the man and best him in a territorial contest of overt masculine power.

The impulse startled him. Even in his amours he never allowed himself to be anything other than self-possessed, and this proprietary attitude towards a woman he didn't even know—and planned to use—was an unwelcome development.

Of course, it couldn't be personal—well, it was, he thought with a slow burn of anger, but it was between him and Gastano. Attractive though she was, the woman was merely a bystander.

Frowning, he noted her reaction to the count's opening remark, scanning her face for emotions as she turned from her contemplation of the lagoon.

Although Rafiq had a hunter's patience, he must have made some slight movement, because the woman looked over the count's shoulder. Her eyes widened momentarily, only to be hastily covered by long lashes.

Not in fear or surprise, he thought, but in warning. A very cool customer, this one. No, he didn't have to concern himself about her feelings; she was fully in command of them.

Narrowly he inspected the regular features highlighted by the silver witchery of starlight. Her sensuous mouth was compressed, her detached expression not altering as Gastano bent his head down to her.

The count's voice was pitched too low for Rafiq to hear what he said, but the tone was unmistakeable—intimate and smoothly caressing.

The woman's brows lifted. 'No, I haven't changed my mind.'

Again the count spoke, and this time Rafiq caught a few words. He stiffened.

Speaking in English, the count had said, 'Come, don't be so angry, my dearest girl,' accompanied by a lingering, significant gaze.

She tossed back a crisp comment and walked past him, her spine straight as she headed for Rafiq.

'Hello,' she said in English, her voice clear and steady. 'I'm Lexie Sinclair. Isn't it a gorgeous evening?' Not giving him time to answer, she turned to include the count and asked in a pleasant tone, 'Do you two know each other?'

Full marks for social skills, Rafiq thought sardonically. Aloud he said, 'Of course.' Without offering a hand, he favoured the other man with a slight unsmiling inclination of his head. 'Gastano.'

'Ah, sir, how delightful to meet you again.' The count's voice was a mixture of impudence and false man-to-man heartiness. 'I must congratulate you on yet another superb investment—I can tell you now that this hotel will be a huge success. I've already had two film stars singing its praises, and at least one minor European royal is planning to bring his latest mistress here for a week's tryst.'

He switched his attention to the woman, letting his eyes linger on her face, and went on in a voice where the impertinence had transmuted into charming ruefulness. 'Alexa, I must introduce you to Rafiq de Courteveille. He is the ruler of this lovely island, and all who live here, you know. But I must warn you to beware of him—he is well known to be a breaker of hearts. Sir, this is Alexa Considine, who prefers to be known as Lexie Sinclair. Perhaps she will tell you why.'

With an ironic smile, he bowed to them both then walked back into the hotel.

Aware of the anger that tightened her neat features, Rafiq took Alexa's arm. Ignoring her startled resistance, he walked her towards the edge of the wide, stone-flagged terrace.

A volatile mixture of irritation laced with apprehension had prompted Lexie's decision to make use of this stranger. If she'd known that he was the hereditary ruler of Moraze she'd never have dared; she'd probably shattered protocol. It had been kind of him to ignore her lack of manners.

So why did she feel that her impulsive approach to him had set something dangerous in motion? Resisting a faint, foolish urge to turn and run, she stole a rapid sideways glance at his face and dragged in a silent breath. A silver wash of starlight emphasised boldly angular features, strong and thrusting and uncompromising.

Dead gorgeous, she thought with involuntary appreciation, her heart picking up speed. In superbly tailored evening clothes he carried himself like an autocrat, his six-foot-several-inches of lean manhood almost intimidating.

Against such steel-hard authority, Felipe's glamorous sophistication suddenly seemed flashy and superficial.

Sedately, she said, 'It's an honour to meet you, sir.'

'My name is Rafiq.' He smiled at her, his dark eyes intent.

Lexie's pulse rate accelerated further, and an odd twist of sensation tightened her stomach. Trying to curb her runaway response, she struggled to remember what she'd read about the man who ruled this small, independent island state.

Not a lot. He didn't make the headlines, or figure largely in the tabloids. Felipe had referred to him contemptuously as 'the tinpot fake prince of a speck of land thousands of miles from civilisation.'

But Felipe's jeering dismissal of the man beside her had been foolish as well as wrong. Rafiq de Couteveille walked in an aura of effortless power based on formidable male assurance.

Her mind jerked away from the memory of the moment that morning when, tired after the long flight from Europe, she'd discovered that Felipe had organised for her to spend the week in a room with him.

It had been a shock. She'd already decided she wasn't in love with Felipe, and by going back to New Zealand she'd be ending their relationship.

The week in Moraze on her own was to have been a holiday, seven days to reorient herself to her real life as a country vet in Northland. Being met by Felipe at the airport had been unexpected. But when he'd swept her off to the hotel he was staying in, and they'd been shown into a suite with flowers everywhere and a bottle of champagne in a silver bucket prominently displayed, she'd realised with dismay and a certain unease that he'd set the scene for seduction.

Still, she'd been civilised about it, and so had Felipe, when she'd told him that no, she wasn't going to join him in any sensual fantasy.

He hadn't argued. Felipe never did. He'd taken her rejection with a smiling shrug, observing that it didn't matter, that he'd sleep on one of the very comfortable sofas. That was when she'd found out that he'd cancelled her booking at her own, much more modest hotel some miles away. It had been impossible to get a room to herself—it was the holiday season and all the hotels were fully booked, an apologetic clerk told her.

It hadn't been the first time Felipe had suggested they make love, but before it had always been with a light touch so she'd never felt pressured.

This time there had been something about his humorously regretful acceptance that didn't ring true; he'd sounded satisfied, almost smug. Oh, she wasn't afraid, but right now she felt a long way from home, and rather vulnerable and wary, whereas before she'd always been at ease with him.

Well, almost always.

He'd talked her into accompanying him to the party, only to abandon her after the first half-hour. It seemed very like punishment.

Yes, she thought—deliberate and rather vindictive. That sense of unease grew. Because she was out of place in this assembly of famous faces she'd seen in newspapers and gossip columns. Others were complete strangers, but they too wore fabulous clothes and even more fabulous jewels, and they all seemed to know each other.

'You are all right?' the man beside her asked in a deep, cool voice that ruffled across her skin like dark velvet.

'Yes, of course.' Goodness, was that her voice? Pitched slightly too high, the words had emerged almost breathlessly.

'Should I apologise for disturbing you and your friend?' Rafiq de Couteveille asked.

'No, not at all,' she said, again too quickly. She fixed her gaze on the lagoon, placid and shimmering beneath the tropical night.

She stole a glance at Rafiq de Couteveille, and a hot shiver worked its way down her spine, igniting her nerves so that she was acutely, almost painfully aware of him. Like her he was looking out across the lagoon, and in the darkness his arrogantly autocratic profile was an uncompromising slash across the star-gemmed sky.

Both he and Felipe were exceedingly good-looking, but the difference between them couldn't have been greater.

Felipe had dazzled her; after the hard work of proving herself to the Illyrians, he'd accepted her without comment, made her laugh, introduced her to interesting people and generally entertained her with a light touch.

And, until she'd been presented with the *fait accompli* of that huge double bed, she'd taken him at face value.

Perhaps she should have seen the signs sooner—like the moment, after they'd been seeing each other for a month or so, when he'd noticed she was tired and told her he could get something that would take away her tiredness…if she wanted him to.

After one glance at her stunned expression he'd laughed softly and with affection, before apologising charmingly, saying that he'd only been testing her.

Then she'd believed him. Now she wondered whether he'd been lying. In spite of seeing so much of him, she really didn't know Felipe at all. Her hands tightened on the balustrade.

'There is something wrong. Can I help?'

Could Rafiq de Couteveille read minds? 'I'm fine,' she said briskly. After all, she didn't know this man either.

'Do you know Gastano well?'

'I've known him for a couple of months,' she said with restraint.

'It appears you are close to becoming engaged to him.'

'What?' He was watching her keenly, those dark eyes uncomfortably piercing. 'I don't know where you got that idea from,' she said more forcefully than she'd intended, startled by her instinctive rejection of the possibility.

His straight brows rose, but his voice was smooth when he said, 'You don't find the idea of taming a man like that intriguing?'

Turning her gaze to the pool and the gracefully curved trunks of the palms beyond, she said abruptly, 'I don't find the idea of taming *any* man intriguing.'

And she stopped, because this was an odd conversation to have with a man she didn't know.

'It's supposed to be a universal female desire,' he observed.

A note in his words told her he was amused—and strangely, she found that a relief. 'Not mine,' she told him brightly. 'What made you think that we were about to become engaged?'

'I heard it somewhere,' he said. 'Perhaps whoever was discussing it misunderstood—or possibly I did. So what *is* your desire?'

The flicker of excitement deep inside her leapt into a flame. He was flirting with her.

She should go back inside. Actually, she should leave this party. But that suite upstairs, with its one huge bed, loomed like a threat. Shrugging off that worry, she smiled up at her companion. Although his lips curved in response, she couldn't see any humour there. He was watching her, his chiselled face enigmatic in the starlight, his expression speculative.

Did he know what was happening to her? Could he feel it too—that keen awareness, the anticipation, hidden yet potent, the whispered instructions she didn't dare obey?

Hastily, before she could react to a treacherous impulse to lift herself onto her toes and kiss his excitingly sensuous mouth, she said demurely, 'Only a foolish woman tells a man her innermost desire.'

'My innermost desire at this moment,' he said, his deep voice investing the conventional words with an edge that sent Lexie's pulse racing into overdrive, 'is to discover if your mouth tastes as good as it looks.'

Lexie froze, her widening eyes taking in his honed features.

His smile twisted into something close to cynicism. 'But not if it goes against your principles.'

'No—well—no,' she stammered, barely able to articulate.

'Then shall we try it?' He took her startled silence for assent, and bent his head to claim her lips in a kiss that was surprisingly gentle.

At first.

But when her bones melted his arms came around her and he pulled her against his lean, powerful body—and all hell broke loose.

That cool, exploring kiss hardened into fierce demand and Lexie burned up in his arms, meeting and matching his frankly sexual hunger. Stunned by an urgent, voluptuous craving, she almost surrendered to the adrenalin raging like a bushfire through her.

She felt the subtle flexion of his body, and knew that he too wanted this—this headstrong need, mindless and sensuous. Desperately, she fought to retain a tiny spark of sanity as a bulwark against the white-hot sensations his experienced kiss summoned inside her.

Yet when he lifted his head and drawled, 'Shall we go further down into the garden?' it took every ounce of her will power to refuse.

In a ragged voice she muttered, 'No.'

He let her go and stepped back. Embarrassed, shocked and angry with herself, she whirled and set off for the bright rectangles of light that indicated the doors onto the terrace.

'One moment.'

Startled into stillness by the decisive command, she stopped and half turned.

He was right behind her. A long-fingered hand lifted to tuck a lock of hair behind her ear, and somehow he managed to turn the simple gesture into a caress that sent more forbidden excitement drumming through her.

'You don't look quite so storm tossed now,' he said, that sardonic smile tilting his lips again as he surveyed her face. 'But a trip to the powder room is advisable, I think.'

'I—yes,' she said, forcing her voice into its usual practical tone. 'Are you coming inside too?'

'Not for a few minutes,' he said gravely. 'My body, alas, is not so easily mastered as yours.'

'Oh.' Hot faced, she took off to the sound of his quiet laughter behind her.

Rafiq watched her go, frowning as his *aide-de-camp* passed her in the doorway, the man's presence breaking in on thoughts that weren't as ordered as he'd have liked.

Dragging his mind away from Lexie's sleek back and the gentle sway of her hips, he said abruptly, 'Yes?'

'Your instructions have been followed.'

'Thank you,' Rafiq said crisply, and turned to go inside. Then he stopped. 'You noticed the woman who passed you on the way in?'

'Yes, sir.' When Rafiq's brows lifted, the younger man expanded, 'She is also under s—' He stopped as Rafiq's brows met over his arrogant nose. Hastily he went on, 'She is staying at the hotel with Count Felipe Gastano.'

He stepped back as another man approached them, saying to Rafiq, 'You're leaving already, sir?'

Rafiq returned the newcomer's smile. He respected any man who'd hauled himself up from poverty and refugee status, and this man—the CEO of the construction firm that had built the new resort—was noted for his honesty and philanthropy. 'I'm afraid I must,' he said. 'I have an early call tomorrow.'

They exchanged pleasantries, but as Rafiq turned to go the older man said, 'And you will consider the matter we discussed previously?'

'I will,' Rafiq told him with remote courtesy. 'But I am unable to make the decision; there must be consultations with the council first.'

The older man said shrewdly, 'I wonder if you will ever regret giving up the power your forebears took for granted?'

Rafiq's broad shoulders lifted in a negligent shrug. 'In

the eyes of the world Moraze might be only a smallish island in the Indian Ocean. But its few-million citizens are as entitled to the privileges and responsibilities of democracy as any other free people, and if they don't want them now they will soon enough. I am a practical man. If I hadn't introduced self-government, power would eventually have been taken away—either from me or from one of my descendants.'

'I wish all rulers were as enlightened,' the other man said. He paused before adding, 'I know my daughter has already thanked you for your magnificent birthday gift, but I must thank you also. I know how rare fire-diamonds are, and that one is superb.'

'It is nothing.' Rafiq dismissed his gift with a smile. 'Freda and I are old friends—and the diamond suits her.'

They shook hands and Rafiq frowned, his mind not on the woman who'd been his lover until six months previously but on Alexa Sinclair Considine, with the gold-burnished hair and the steady gaze, and a mouth that summoned erotic fantasies.

And her relationship with a man he loathed and despised.

She was no longer in the room, Rafiq realised after one comprehensive glance around the large salon. And neither was Felipe Gastano.

CHAPTER TWO

Up in the palatial bedroom, Lexie could still hear the faint sound of music. Moraze was as glorious as its discreet publicity promised——a large island, dominated by a long-extinct chain of volcanoes ground down by aeons of wind and weather to become a jagged range of mountains bordering a vast plateau area.

Just before landing the previous day Lexie had leaned forward to peer at the green-gold grasslands. She'd hoped for a glimpse of the famed wild horses of Moraze, only to sink back disappointed when lush coastal lands came into view, vividly patched with green sugar cane and the bright colours of flower farms.

Now, standing at the glass doors onto the balcony, she remembered that the island's heraldic animal was a rearing horse wearing a crown. Her mind skipped from the horse to the man it signified, and she lifted her hands to suddenly burning cheeks.

That kiss had been scandalously disturbing, so different from any other she'd ever experienced that it had overwhelmed her.

Why? Yes, Rafiq de Couteveille was enormously attractive, with that compelling air of dangerous assurance, but she was accustomed to attractive men. Her sister Jacoba was married to one, and Marco's older brother was just as stunning in a slightly sterner way. Yet neither of them had summoned so much as an extra heartbeat from her.

It wasn't just his leanly aquiline features, boldly sculpted into a tough impression of force and power, that had made such an impression. Although Felipe Gastano was actually better-looking, he didn't have an ounce of Rafiq's dangerous charisma. She couldn't imagine Felipe on a warhorse, leading his warriors into battle, but it was very easy to picture Rafiq de Couteveille doing exactly that.

Or she could see him as a corsair, she thought, heart quickening when her too-active imagination visualised him with a cutlass between his teeth as he swung over the side of a vessel...

According to the hotel publicity, in the eighteenth century the Indian Ocean had been the haunt of buccaneers. Moraze had been threatened by them, and had also used them in the struggle to keep its independence. Eventually the corsairs had been brought to heel, and Moraze's rulers were at last able to give up the dangerous double game they'd been forced to play.

But no doubt the corsairs had left their genes in the bloodlines of the people of Moraze. Certainly Rafiq looked like a warrior—stern, hard and ruthless if the occasion demanded it.

However, fantasising about him wasn't any help in dealing with her most pressing problem. Frowning, she stepped back inside. What the hell was she to do?

She wished she could trust Felipe to sleep on the sofa,

but she didn't. If she chose the bed, she suspected he might see it as an invitation for him to join her, and she did *not* want an undignified struggle when he finally decided to come up for the night.

Making up her mind, she pulled the light coverlet from the foot of the bed, grabbed a pillow, changed into cotton trousers and a shirt and curled up on the sofa.

She woke to music—from outside, she realised as she disentangled herself from the coverlet. Vaguely apprehensive, she glanced towards the closed bedroom door and grimaced. Once she'd finally fallen asleep, Rafiq de Couteveille had taken over her dreams to such an extent that she was possessed by an odd, aching restlessness.

The light she'd left on glowed softly, barely bright enough to show her a note someone had slipped under the door. Heart thudding, she untangled herself and ran across to retrieve it.

My dear girl, she read, *I am sorry to have inconvenienced you. As it upset you so much to think of sharing a room with me, I have thrown myself on the sympathy of good friends who have a suite here. Because I do not trust myself with you.*

Felipe had signed it with an elaborate *F.*

Lexie let out a long breath. She could have slept in the bed without fear, it seemed. It was thoughtful of Felipe.

Or perhaps, she thought, remembering the way he'd more or less ignored her at the party last night, this too was a little punishment?

Surely he wouldn't be so petty?

It didn't matter; the clerk had promised her a room of her own tomorrow—today, she amended after a glance at the clock. Felipe's consideration should have appeased her, but his assumption that he could manipulate her into bed had crossed a boundary, and she knew it was time to tell him that their friendship would never develop any further.

Surprised at the relief that flooded her, she realised she'd been resisting a creeping sense of wrongness ever since he'd offered to buy drugs for her.

So her decision had nothing to do with the fact that he seemed far less vital—almost faded—next to the vital, hard-edged charisma of the man who'd kissed her on the terrace.

Felipe's kisses had been warm and pleasant, but conveyed nothing like the raw charge of Rafiq's…

'Oh, *stop* it!' she commanded her inconvenient memory.

Irritated, she poured herself some water to drink, and carried it across to the glass door leading onto the balcony.

The music that had somehow tangled her dreams in its sensuous beat had fallen silent now, the only sounds the sibilant whisper of a breeze in the casuarinas, the sleepy hush of small waves on the beach, and the muted thunder of breakers against the reef. As far as she could see the lagoon spread before her like a shadowy masquerade cloak spangled with silver.

She drank deeply, willing herself to relax, to enjoy the breeze that flirted with her hair, its hint of salt and flower perfumes mingling with a faint, evocative scent of spices, of ancient mysteries and secrets hidden from the smiling beauty of daylight.

It was almost dawn, although as yet no light glowed in the eastern sky. Feeling like the only person in the world, she took a deep breath and moved farther out onto the balcony.

The hair on the nape of her neck lifted, and unthinkingly

she stepped back into the darkness of the overhang, senses straining as her eyes darted back and forth to search out what had triggered that primitive instinct.

Don't be an idiot, she told herself uneasily, there's no one out there—and even if there were it would be some sort of night watchman.

Moving slowly and quietly, she eased into her room and pulled the glass door shut, locking it and making sure there was no gap in the curtains.

But even then it was difficult to dispel that eerie sense of being watched. She marched across to the bathroom and set the glass down, washed her face, and then wondered how she was going to get back to sleep.

Half an hour later she gave up the attempt and decided to email her sister Jacoba.

Only to discover that for some reason the internet link wouldn't work. Thoroughly disgruntled, she closed down her laptop and drank another glass of water.

It seemed that Felipe had decided to continue his charade of rejection. After breakfast in her room the butler hand-delivered a note that told her Gastano had business to attend to in Moraze's capital, and would see her that evening.

Suddenly light-hearted, Lexie arranged the transfer of her luggage to a new room, then organised a trip up to the mountains, eager to see the results of the world-famous bird-protection programme.

It was a surprise to find herself alone in the small tourist van with a woman who informed her she was both driver and guide.

'Just you today, *m'selle,*' she confirmed cheerfully. 'I know all about this place, so, if you got any questions, you ask.'

And know about Moraze she did, dispensing snippets of information all the more intriguing for having a strong personal bias. Lexie plied her with questions, and once they reached the high grasslands she looked eagerly for signs of the horses.

'You like horses?' the driver asked.

'Very much. I'm a vet,' Lexie told her.

'OK, I tell you about the horses.'

Lexie soaked up her information, much of which concerned the legendary relationship between the horses and the ruler.

'As long as the horses flourish,' the guide finished on the approach to a sweeping corner, 'Our Emir will also, and so will Moraze.'

She spoke as though it were written law. Lexie asked curiously, 'Why do you call him the Emir?'

'It's kind of a joke, because the first de Couteveille was a duke in France. He got into trouble there, and after a couple of years of roaming in exile he found Moraze. He brought an Arabian princess with him.' She gave a thousand-watt smile. 'Their descendants have kept Moraze safe for hundreds of years, so you better believe we look after those horses! We don't want anyone else taking over our island, thank you very much.'

Lexie gasped with alarm as the guide suddenly jerked the wheel. The van skidded, the world turned upside down, and amidst a harsh cacophony of sounds Lexie was flung forward against the seatbelt. It locked across her, the force driving the breath from her lungs, so that she dragged air into them with a painful grunt.

The laboured sound of the engine and a strong smell of petrol forced her to ignore her maltreated ribs. A cool little wind played with her hair, blowing it around her face. She forced her eyes open and saw grass, long and golden, rustling in the breeze.

The car had buried its nose in the low bank on one side of the road, and when she tried her door it refused to open. She turned her head, wincing at a sharp pain in her neck, to see the driver slumped behind the wheel. The woman's harsh breathing filled the vehicle.

'I have to turn off the engine,' Lexie said aloud. If she didn't it might catch fire.

Easing herself around, she freed the seatbelt and groped for the key. She could just reach it. With shaking fingers, she twisted rapidly, hugely relieved when the engine sputtered into silence.

Now she had to see if the driver was all right. If it was a heart attack she could at least give CPR. But first she had to get out, which meant crawling over the poor woman, possibly making any injuries worse…

She reached for the driver's wrist, hugely relieved when the pulse beat strongly beneath her shaking fingers. And then she heard the distant throb of a powerful engine, a sound she identified as a helicopter.

The pilot must have seen the wrecked car because the chopper altered course. The clack-clack-clack of the engine filled the air, and seconds later the craft landed in a haze of dust and wind. Immediately a man leapt down, ducking to avoid the rotors as he ran towards her. Lexie put her hand up to her eyes and closed them, then looked again, blinking hard.

Even at this distance she knew him. Rafiq de Couteveille—the man who had kissed her only last night…

Stunned, her stomach hollow, Lexie watched him yank

open the driver's door and crouch beside her. After one quick glance at the unconscious woman, he transferred his gaze to Lexie's face.

'You are all right?' he demanded, pitching his voice so she could hear him above the noise of the helicopter.

Lexie nodded, ignoring the sharp stab of maltreated muscles in her neck. 'I think she might have had a heart attack.'

He bent his attention to the crumpled woman beside her. Was he a doctor? No, he didn't look like a doctor.

The driver stirred and muttered something in the local Creole French, then opened her eyes.

'Don't worry,' Rafiq de Couteville said. 'We'll have you both out soon.'

No sooner said than done; within a few minutes the driver was free and being carried across to the chopper by two men, and Rafiq was saying, 'Let me help you.'

'I can manage, thank you.'

But he eased her past the wheel, his strong arms gentle and controlled. In spite of the shivers racking her when he set her carefully on her feet, her breath was shallow and her colour high.

And all she could think of was that she must look a real guy. 'Thank you,' she said as crisply as she could.

Something flickered in the dark eyes—green, she realised in the clear light of the Moraze day. Not just ordinary green, either—the pure, dense green of the very best pounamu, New Zealand's prized native jade.

'So we meet again,' he said with an ironic twist to his beautifully chiselled mouth.

He was too close. Taking an automatic step backwards, she turned slightly away, her brows meeting for a second as another twinge of pain tightened the muscles in her neck.

Sharply he asked, 'Where are you hurt?'

'I'm not—the seatbelt was just a bit *too* efficient.' Her smile faded as she asked anxiously, 'Is the driver all right?'

'I think so.'

Lexie swallowed to ease a suddenly dry throat. 'I'm so glad you happened to be passing.'

He responded courteously, 'And so, Alexa Considine, am I.'

'Lexie. My name is Lexie,' she told him. 'From New Zealand,' she added idiotically.

She shivered, then stiffened as he picked her up and strode towards the chopper.

'I can walk,' she muttered.

'I doubt it. You're in shock. Keep your head down.'

Her face turned into his shoulder; she inhaled his dark, male scent. He ducked, and it was with faces almost pressed together that they headed for the chopper door. Lexie shut her eyes.

She felt safe, she thought raggedly—safer than she had ever felt in her life.

Which was odd, because every instinct she possessed was shouting a warning. Somehow she'd managed to forget that he had his own particular scent—faint, yet hugely evocative. And although her ribs were still complaining, memories flooded back in sensory overload as the remembered impact of that kiss burned through every cell in her body.

The noise of the helicopter's engines thundered through her, turning her shivers into shudders; by the time the chopper lifted off, she was white to the lips.

At least she'd managed not to throw up, she thought distantly after they landed in the grounds of a large building in the capital city.

The following hours passed in a blur of movement and noise, at last relieved by blessed peace when she was delivered to a solitary bed in a small, cool room overlooking the sea. She looked up from the pillows as Rafiq de Couteveille came in with a slender woman at his side—the doctor who'd supervised her tests.

'How are you now?' he asked.

'Better, thank you.' Except that her throat had turned to sand. Huskily she asked, 'How is the driver?'

'Like you, she doesn't seem hurt apart from mild shock,' Rafiq told her.

'Does she know what happened?'

He scanned her face with hard green eyes. 'An animal apparently ran out in front of the coach.'

'I hope it wasn't hurt,' she said quietly.

The woman beside him smiled. 'Probably not as much as you are. Our animals run fast. Although you have bruises, you do not have anything cracked or broken. However, you're still suffering a mild case of shock, so it seems a good idea to keep you in here for tonight.'

Rafiq de Couteveille asked, 'Is there anyone I should contact?'

If her sister Jacoba heard about this she'd be on a jet to Moraze immediately. Crisply, Lexie said, 'No. I'll be fine, and I presume there's no reason why I shouldn't see out the rest of my holiday?'

He looked at the doctor, who said, 'None at all, with a few precautions. I'll tell you about those tomorrow before you leave hospital.'

'I do need to notify someone about where I am,' she

objected, feeling rather as though someone had run over her with a steamroller.

'I will contact the count,' Rafiq de Couteveille said calmly. 'The doctor feels that you need to be left alone tonight, so don't expect visitors.' When Lexie frowned he told her, 'The hotel is sending along toiletries and clothes. I will leave you now. Do everything you are told to do, and don't worry about anything.'

Silenced by the authority in his tone and bearing, Lexie watched him stride out of the room beside the doctor, tall and utterly sure of himself, the superbly tailored light suit revealing a body that made her foolish heart increase speed dramatically. How could one man pack so much punch?

And how had he appeared up on those grassy plains—literally from out of the blue?

Like a genie from a bottle, she thought, and gave an involuntary smile, because the image was so incongruous. Rafiq de Couteveille bore all the hallmarks of an alpha male—it would be a very clever magician who managed to confine him.

And it would take a special sort of woman to match that impressive male charisma—someone elegant, sophisticated, worldly.

Someone completely unlike Lexie Sinclair, a vet from New Zealand who'd never even had a lover!

Which inevitably brought more memories of that kiss—explosive, exciting and still capable of causing a delicious agitation that temporarily made her forget her tender ribs and stiff neck.

It almost seemed like fate, she thought dreamily, that they should meet again…

Oh, how ridiculous! Coincidences happened all the

time—everyone had stories of the most amazing ones that meant nothing at all.

Forget about him, she told herself sternly.

When she eased out of bed the following morning an inspection of her body revealed some mild bruising over her ribs. She was also stiff, although movement would ease that. However the shakiness that had startled her after the accident was gone.

And although the doctor was cautious she said there was no reason why she shouldn't leave, cautioning her to take things easy until the bruises had faded and she felt completely well.

So she dressed in the outfit that had arrived from the hotel the previous evening with her toiletries, and sat down rather limply on the chair. Presumably Felipe would come and get her, and she just didn't feel like dealing with him at the moment.

A knock at the door made her brace herself. 'Come in,' she called, getting to her feet and squaring her shoulders.

But it wasn't Felipe. When Rafiq de Couteveille walked in, his lithe form immaculate in superbly tailored casual clothes, her heart performed an odd gyration in her chest, quivering as it finally came to rest.

'Ready to leave?' he asked, dark eyes cool and measuring.

Later she'd wonder why on earth she hadn't asked him what he was doing there.

'Yes, of course.' Oddly breathless, she picked up the small bag with her clothes from yesterday.

'You will be more comfortable once you get home,' he said calmly. At her hesitation, his brows met for a second across his nose. 'Come—they'll be wanting this room soon.'

'I can't ask you to drive me back to the hotel,' she said inanely. 'Felipe—?'

'But you aren't asking me,' he pointed out with a smile that pierced her fragile shell of independence.

When she still didn't move he held out an imperative hand.

With a meekness entirely foreign to her, Lexie handed over her bag.

CHAPTER THREE

COOL, firm fingers gripped Lexie's elbow. Rafiq said, 'Shall I ring for a wheelchair?'

'Of course not,' she spluttered, and started walking.

But once out beneath Moraze's brilliant sun she was glad to sink into the air-conditioned comfort of the waiting vehicle.

He took the wheel, which surprised her; she'd have presumed the ruler of a place with several million inhabitants would have a limousine with a chauffeur. Instead he drove a late-model car, sleek, and with all the accoutrements of luxury.

Hanging on to the remnants of her composure, she said steadily, 'This is very kind of you.'

'It is the least I can do,' he said, adding with a smile that barely tucked in the corners of his sculpted mouth, 'We value our tourists. It is a pity your trip to the jungle was cut short. When you are fully recovered I will take you there.'

Lexie stared straight ahead, refusing to allow herself to feel any excitement at the prospect. They were passing beneath an avenue of tall palms, and the shadows of their long, slender trunks flashing across her eyes set up such an unpleasant rhythm that she turned her head away.

Unfortunately this gave her an extremely good view of Rafiq de Couteveille's profile in all its autocratic purity. Whatever interesting meld of races and cultures had given him that face, it was disturbingly beautiful in a very masculine way—a compelling amalgam of angles and curves and hard-honed lines that spoke of formidable power.

And perhaps just a hint of cruelty? She would not, she thought with an inner shiver, closing her eyes, want to make an enemy of him.

His voice broke into her thoughts. 'Here, take these.'

Eyes flying open, she realised he was holding out his sunglasses. 'I can't—you'll need them,' she said, unwilling to wear something so intimately connected to him.

He shrugged. 'You are not accustomed to this sun. I am.'

And very much accustomed to getting your own way, she thought dryly.

But then rulers were notorious for that. Reluctantly she accepted the spectacles and perched them on the end of her nose.

They made an immense difference. She said quietly, 'Thank you. I'm not usually so wimpish.'

'You are too harsh on yourself. There is a difference between being fragile and being a wimp, and an accident always leaves one shaken. Why don't you put your head back and rest quietly?'

It was couched as a question, but clearly he expected her to obey. And because it was simpler she did, waiting for the hum of the engine to calm her.

Only to find the impact of the man next to her negated

any soothing effect. Rafiq de Couteveille got to her in a way no other man ever had, his presence alerting unsuspected sensory receptors in her mind and body, so that everything seemed suddenly more vivid, more exhilarating, more *more*, she thought with a surge of apprehension.

She didn't need this. Because she'd spent so much of her time studying, she'd missed out on the social aspect of university life. But she'd watched with considerable bewilderment when heartbroken friends suffered agonies over young men she'd considered shallow and inconsiderate.

Eventually she'd decided there had to be something missing in her. Possibly growing up without a father had somehow stunted her response to men.

In a way, that was why she'd let herself be beguiled by Felipe. It had been such a relief to discover that she *could* enjoy flirting with a man!

But this—this was entirely different—a driving, uncontrollable reaction that was dangerous and altogether too tantalising.

If this was how lust started, she thought wryly, she could at last understand why it was so difficult to resist. She catalogued her symptoms: racing heartbeat, a kind of softening of the muscles, a fluttering in her stomach that hovered between apprehension and excitement, a keen attentiveness and heightened physical responses.

And an involuntary reaction to the memory of his mouth on hers that still embarrassed and shocked her.

Yes, it sounded like the first stages of attraction, all right. And of course it was doomed, because Rafiq de Couteveille was a kind of king, even though he didn't have any title.

No, not a king—a sheikh, she decided, watching him

through her lashes. His profile was strongly marked and arrogant, and when he walked she could almost hear the swish of robes about that lean, powerfully muscled body. In spite of the superb tailoring of his clothes and his luxurious car, there was something untamed about him, as though he lived by a more elemental code.

Beneath the sophisticated exterior he was a warrior, and she sensed a warrior's uncompromising determination. Clearly he was of French descent, but Rafiq was an Arabic name, and she'd bet that Moraze's ruler had familial links to both cultures.

'Are you feeling all right?'

Lexie's eyes flew open. 'Yes, fine, thank you,' she said a little disjointedly.

Rafiq snatched a sideways glance at his passenger, then fixed his gaze on the road ahead. Her exquisite skin was still pale, and her ribs would probably be painful beneath the seatbelt. 'It's not very far now.'

Smoky eyes hidden by his sunglasses, she leaned forward, a frown showing in her tone. 'I don't remember this part of the road.'

Rafiq shrugged. 'Possibly because you have not seen it before. When the doctor and I discussed your condition, we agreed it would be better for you to spend the next few days in a place with more peace than the hotel could provide. So you will be staying with me.'

And he waited with interest and a certain amount of anticipation for her response.

Her head swung around. She snapped off the sunglasses to glare at him, eyes gleaming the blue of a Spanish sword blade, her lush mouth compressed in outrage. 'Why wasn't I included in this discussion?' she demanded tautly.

'It wasn't necessary,' Rafiq replied, intrigued in spite of himself.

She could be a consummate actress. And she could be truly in love with Gastano. In which case, she'd thank him one day for this abduction.

After scrutinising him as though she couldn't believe what she'd heard, her delectable mouth opened, then closed again, to bite back what were clearly intemperate words.

Fully aware of her seething resentment, Rafiq kept his eyes on the road ahead and waited.

In the end she said through gritted teeth, 'There is no need to treat me like a halfwit just because I've been in a minor—a *very* minor—accident.'

'I'm sure your family would agree with me that you need a few days' respite after a nasty experience,' he said blandly. 'Should I contact them to check?'

'No!'

'Why not?'

After a second's hesitation, she said reluctantly, 'My sister is six months' pregnant. She'd insist on flying out here, and the trip would exhaust her. I'm sure you and the doctor are only thinking of my wellbeing, but I'm perfectly capable of looking after myself. You don't have to feel any sort of responsibility for me.'

'Possibly not, but the hotel management said they were not equipped to deal with someone convalescing, and it was agreed that this was the best solution.' He allowed that to sink in, ignoring her mutinous expression to finish, 'You will spend several days at my home—which is big enough to give you all the privacy you desire—and once the doctor has given you the all-clear you can go back to the hotel.'

After considering this she said briefly, 'In that case, I should let Count Gastano know where I'll be.'

Rafiq controlled the curl of his lip, despising himself for wanting to believe she was just a naive New Zealand girl entangled by the count's deceptive charm. His brows drew together. This wildfire, highly inconvenient attraction couldn't—*wouldn't*—be allowed to distract him from his reason for keeping her tucked safely away where she couldn't contact the self-titled count.

'Gastano has already been told about your accident.' Rafiq let that sink in, then said, 'I believe he has business here that will keep him occupied for some days. Then you can join him again.'

Steadily she said, 'It doesn't sound as though I have any choice in the matter.'

'I'm sorry if my decision conflicts with your independence.'

'Well, it does.' Her voice was crisp and cool. 'However, I've never thought banging my head against a wall was a sensible way of working through a situation. Thank you for the hospitality. I'm sure you won't mind if I avail myself of it for as short a time as possible.'

Lexie hoped the final snide comment might pierce his armour-plated inflexibility, but when he gave her a smile that almost banished her justifiable resentment she realised he was still fully in control.

And that smile was an epiphany—filled with charm and sexual magnetism, it was the sort of smile that led to broken hearts and despair.

Grimly, Lexie concentrated on the scenery until her body stopped singing.

Fortunately the scenery was worth looking at, with everything that was exotic about the tropics—brilliant sky, deep aquamarine lagoon, vivid flowers and the intense green of the countryside, coconut palms bending gracefully over white sand, and mountains purple with heat haze...

Determined not to be impressed, she decided it was just like a picture in a travel magazine.

Besides, if it came to a competition, New Zealand had some of the best beaches in the world. And pretty good mountains too, jutting into as blue a sky, and displaying every bit as much boldness and drama as these peaks did.

The man beside her said, 'I have never been to New Zealand, but I believe it's very beautiful.'

Was he a mind reader? 'It is,' she said woodenly, and let the conversation lie there, dead on the floor.

His smile was wry. 'So what particular part of the country do you come from?'

'I grew up in Northland.'

'It's a long way from there to Moraze.'

Dampening down her impulse to use the manners her mother had drilled into her, she confined her answer to a few noncommittal words. 'Indeed it is.'

If he had the nerve to mention that kiss, she'd—she'd tell him straight it was a one-off, an indiscretion she had no intention of repeating.

He didn't. Instead he asked, 'Do you specialise in a certain sort of animal in your veterinary practice?'

'Domestic animals,' she said, adding reluctantly, 'But it's a country practice, so I also deal with a lot of farm animals.'

'Horses?'

'Sometimes,' she admitted.

How did he know she was a vet?

She tried to remember where her profession was given

in her passport, then recalled writing it in the arrival form she'd filled in as they came towards Moraze.

So he'd checked her travel documents—or more likely had ordered someone else to check them.

All right; security was a concern to those who were rich and famous enough to attract obsessive or downright dangerous people. Nevertheless, the thought of anyone poking around in her life gave Lexie an uneasy feeling.

Keeping her gaze defiantly on the view outside, she was about to observe tartly that as he knew all about her there was no need for further conversation, when she realised she couldn't be rude to a man who'd gone out of his way to be kind to her after the accident. Also, he was going to be her host for a few days.

She searched for something innocuous to say and finally came up with a subject. 'I went diving the day I arrived. The reef fishes are absolutely gorgeous—like living jewels.'

'You are interested in jewels?' he commented dispassionately.

Perhaps that was the way everyone referred to the fish here and he found it trite. Well, she didn't care.

Of course, Moraze was famous for the rare and exquisite—and extremely valuable—fire-diamonds found in gravel beds washed down from the mountains. Perhaps he thought she was hinting; no, how could he?

'Most people are. Off Northland's east coast we have a very interesting mix of sea life. A warm current sweeps south from the tropics, and we get a mixture of tropical and temperate fauna.'

OK, so she sounded like something out of a textbook, and was probably boring him to bits. It served him right. If he'd taken her to the hotel, instead of conspiring with the doctor behind her back, he'd have been rid of her by now.

'It sounds most intriguing,' he said smoothly, returning the waves of a small group of children walking down the road.

A few metres further on he turned into a drive and the big car passed between gates that had slid back silently at the press of an unknown button. Lexie looked around for a sentry box, but clearly security nowadays was much more technical and far less conspicuous. Ahead, the drive began to climb steeply through a tangle of greenery.

'We're almost there,' Rafiq told her.

He lived in a castle. Perched on the edge of a cliff overlooking the lagoon, it frowned down over a scene as beautiful as it was deserted.

Lexie drew a sharp breath. 'I don't know much about the architecture of castles, but that looks like something out of the Middle East.'

'It's a mixture of Oriental and European styles.'

The car eased to a halt outside a huge set of what appeared to be bronze doors, sculpted and ornate, with a grid of iron spikes poised above to grind down in case of an attack. Rafiq switched off the engine.

In the silence the sound of the waves on the reef echoed in Lexie's ears. A manservant came swiftly out through a side door and went to the boot of the car, and one of the big bronze doors swung slowly open.

Rafiq looked at her, heavy-lidded eyes narrowing as he scanned her face. 'Moraze was known to Arab sailors, but because it wasn't on their trade routes and had nothing they wanted they rarely came this way. The first settlers were led by a distant ancestor of mine, a French nobleman who had the temerity to conduct an affair with his monarch's much-prized mistress. Nowhere in Europe was safe, so he travelled farther afield, and eventually found refuge here with a somewhat motley crew of adventurers and sailors and their women.'

Fascinated, Lexie said, 'I wouldn't have thought the King of France's mandate stretched this far.'

He smiled, and the skin at the back of her neck tightened, lifting the tiny hairs there. For a second she thought she saw his ancestor, proud and gallant and tough as he shepherded that motley crew to Moraze.

Rafiq told her, 'By then it wasn't the French king he was concerned about. On his travels my forebear stole an Arabian sheikh's most precious jewel—his daughter— and as she was more than happy to be stolen they needed a refuge they could defend.'

'When did all this happen?'

'Several hundred years ago.'

Fascinated, she asked, 'What happened to the French king's mistress?'

He looked surprised. 'I believe she was married off to some elderly duke. Why?'

'I just wondered,' she said. 'I hope she liked that elderly duke.'

'I don't think anyone ever enquired,' he told her dryly.

As though bored by the discussion, he got out and came around to open her door. With the same automatic courtesy he took her arm as they went up the steps and through the door into a vast, tiled hall. She'd expected grim stone inside, but the far end of the hall was high glass doors that opened out onto a terrace bordered by shrubs and trees.

'Oh, how lovely!' Lexie stopped without thinking.

Rafiq said smoothly, 'I'm glad you like it. Let me show you up to your room.'

The staircase was wide and shallow, but by the time she reached the top her ribs were letting Lexie know they'd had a difficult time recently, and the tide of anticipation had receded, leaving her flat and exhausted. Exasperated by her weakness, she had to force her legs to take the final few steps.

He left her with a maid at the door. 'Your clothes have been brought here from the hotel. Cari will show you where everything is,' he said, and that hard green gaze rested for several charged seconds on her face. 'You look a little pale; I suggest a rest, perhaps even a nap, then some refreshments when you are ready for them.'

Her room turned out to be more like a suite—something from an *Arabian Nights* tale of love lost and won, she thought, gazing at the huge bed covered in sleek silk, its sensuously curved headboard picked out in gilding. Translucent curtains softened the light from the sea, and the silk Chinese rug was in restful shades of blue, green and cream that echoed the colours of the ocean without competing with them.

And everywhere—in the window recesses, on the exquisitely carved desk, in a massive urn on the floor—were flowers, mainly white and cream, their scent sweet and seductive on the warm air.

Lexie felt totally out of place in her white jeans and simple tee-shirt. This room looked as though it had been built for a languorous concubine in flowing, transparent robes, a woman with only one aim in life—to please her lord.

That thought tightened something deep inside her. Hot cheeked, she thought with defiance that the room—and the maid—would just have to get used to her downmarket wardrobe. Apart from her flame-coloured silk and a couple of simple dinner dresses, she'd brought only holiday clothes to Moraze.

The maid spoke English reasonably well, and after showing Lexie the dressing room, took her into a splendid marble fantasy of a bathroom dominated by a huge, free-standing bath.

'Heavens! It's almost a swimming pool!' Lexie exclaimed.

Cari laughed, and gestured at a pierced marble screen, almost hidden by pots of lush greenery. 'Behind there is the shower—very modern,' she said eagerly. 'Perhaps you would like one now before your rest?'

'I would very much, thank you.'

Sighing happily, Lexie stepped into the shower and washed herself, carefully skimming the sore spots. Since her sister had married into the Illyrian aristocracy Lexie had become accustomed to luxury. But Rafiq's castle, she thought as the water swept away her aches, was something else again, its exotic beauty out of this world.

Just like Moraze.

Rafiq's story about his ancestors had added to the island's unusual charm. With herds of elegant wild horses and rare, exquisite fire-diamonds, transcendent beauty and isolation, Moraze was a fairy-tale place, a spellbound island that might disappear overnight into an enchanted mist…

Scoffing at her unusual flight of fancy, Lexie turned off the water and wrapped herself in one of the embroidered towels the maid had placed for her.

A rest would put paid to these feverish fantasies, she

thought stoutly, wincing as she rubbed herself down. She inspected her bruises, then shrugged. Because of the seatbelt she'd got off lightly, and she was a fast healer, so the marks would soon be gone.

Yet it wasn't just her ribs that had had a workout; her heart felt ominously fragile, as though it was under attack.

When she arrived back in the bedroom the maid had drawn back the covers on the bed; smiling, she pointed out a waiting jug of water and a glass. Lexie waited until she'd left the room before climbing gratefully into that enormous, decadent bed.

She slept deeply, without dreams, for almost an hour. Rubbing her eyes, she swung her feet onto the floor and realised she felt hugely better.

'Almost normal,' she said with satisfaction, examining her clothes. Carefully hung in the dressing room, they looked rather pathetic. As well as the orange silk dress, Jacoba had insisted on buying her several resort-style outfits, but what on earth did a reluctant guest in a castle wear?

And should she substitute a complete make-up for her usual lip-gloss?

No; she didn't want to look as though she was trying to attract…well, anyone.

Defiantly ignoring a quickening of her pulse, she chose one of Jacoba's purchases. The relaxed cotton trousers sat lightly on her hips to emphasise her long legs, and the silk shirt's subdued pattern repeated the soft camel colour of the trousers. The cosmetics she left at a tinted moisturiser and some lip-gloss.

Before she rang the bell for the maid she walked across to a window and looked out. Sheer stone walls fell away from the windows that opened onto an infinity of sea and sky, framed by the panelled white shutters.

The maid escorted her downstairs again and out onto the long terrace, where Rafiq de Couteveille sat in the shade of a spreading tree that carpeted the flagstones with brilliant purple petals. The sultry scent of gardenias hung heavy and erotic in the lazy air. Lexie's betraying heartbeat kicked up another gear when her host lifted his impressive height from a chair and inspected her with one of his intent, penetrating surveys. Prickles of awareness shot down her spine.

'Yes, that's better,' he said, and indicated the chair beside him. 'Are your ribs painful?'

'Only when I twist,' she told him, her voice as prosaic as she could make it. She avoided that piercing scrutiny by lowering herself into the chair. 'How is the driver?'

The sooner she got better, the faster she'd get away from this man. He attracted her in ways that scared her.

Like Jacoba, her half-sister, Rafiq possessed more than superficial good looks. Jacoba's character illuminated her stunning face, and Rafiq's formidable authority endowed his aquiline features with strength as well as charisma. It was a potent combination that made Lexie feel very vulnerable.

Rafiq told her, 'She is at home with her family, recovering fast. She sent her apologies, and her thanks for the flowers you ordered for her.'

'I'd have liked to see her, but they wouldn't let me.'

He frowned. 'The doctor told me you had to rest as much as possible.'

'I will.' Carefully steering her thoughts away from the personal, she straightened her shoulders and laboured on with brittle composure. 'This must be a very old building. Is it where your ancestors originally settled?'

'No, they built the much grimmer fortress that now overlooks the capital city. This began as a watchtower, one of a chain along the coasts that were always kept manned.'

'That Arabian princess's father must have had a long arm,' she said flippantly.

He shrugged. 'Moraze has always needed good defences.'

'I didn't realise there had been pirates on the Indian Ocean,' she admitted. 'I really don't know much about its history.'

'Why should you? If you are interested I have books I can lend you, but like most histories it is long and bloody and dominated by force. Through good luck and considerable cunning, my ancestors kept the island safe until eventually the corsairs—and other threats—were either assimilated or crushed.' He looked up as a maid appeared with a tray. 'I noticed that you drank tea at the hospital, so I ordered that, but say so if you'd prefer coffee or a cold drink.'

He noticed too much.

And oddly, that last meeting with Felipe popped into Lexie's brain. How much had Rafiq seen or heard?

She should have realised that the count's practised charm hid your average, garden-variety wolf, she thought ironically. Then she wouldn't be feeling quite so foolish.

Oh well. She'd learned something her friends at university could have told her years ago: some men weren't to be trusted.

'Tea will be lovely, thank you,' she said sedately.

What followed was all on the surface, the conversation of two people who knew little of each other, yet Lexie sensed undercurrents. Partly it was a feeling of something held back, of being swept into events over which she had no control.

But most of her tension, she decided with rueful frankness, was rooted in the explosive memory of that kiss.

CHAPTER FOUR

WARINESS tightened Lexie's skin. Unable to resist the temptation, she stole a look at Rafiq, colouring when she met greenstone eyes slightly narrowed against the sun and clinical in their detachment. A superstitious shiver ran through her—fierce, uncaged, almost desperate, forcing her to glance away hastily before those perceptive eyes homed in on her inner turmoil.

What would it take to break through his iron control?

More than she was prepared to risk, she thought bleakly. His air of authority wasn't just a family heirloom handed down from hundreds of years of unquestioned rule. Sure, some of it might be due to the potent effect of strongly handsome features backed by wealth and power, but underpinning it was an indefinable aura of masculine competence.

This man could make a woman ache with desire and scream her satisfaction in his arms.

Lexie's cup jangled musically in the saucer as she set both down, and her tone was a little too abrupt when she asked the first thing that came into her head. 'How long have you ruled Moraze?'

'For ten years,' he said readily enough, adding, 'Since I was twenty. My father died young.'

'I'm sorry,' she said quietly, turning her head to admire the crimson blossoms of a hibiscus close by.

Rafiq's gaze sharpened. Those clear-cut features might appear to reveal every emotion, but her silences were enigmatic.

So her father was a sore point.

Well, he admitted silently, if his sire had been notorious for his perfidy and cruelty, he too would avoid mentioning him.

He waited before saying, 'Life can be cruel. Tell me, what decided you to become a vet?' And he watched her through half-closed lashes, noting the tiny, almost unnoticeable signs of her relaxation.

She answered his question without hesitation. 'I love animals, and I wanted to be able to do something for them.'

'Very altruistic of you,' he drawled, irritated by her pat answer.

She flashed him a direct look, following it with a cool, 'Of course, it pays well too.'

'The training is long and very expensive, I believe.'

'I managed,' she returned, her level tone a contrast to the challenge in her eyes. 'I was lucky—I had a regular holiday job, and my sister helped a lot.'

Jacoba had worked as a model from the time she turned sixteen, determined to earn enough to care for their ill mother. Her extremely successful career had also helped with Lexie's tuition and boarding fees.

In spite of Jacoba's insistence that it wasn't necessary, Lexie was slowly reimbursing her. The past year's leave of absence had meant a hiatus in her repayments, but she'd be able to start again when she got back home.

No doubt Rafiq de Couteveille had swanned around

enjoying himself with some easy option at college. Not for him the worry of sordid, boring things like where the next meal was coming from, or whether a good daughter would be staying at home to care for her mother rather than putting her own ambitions first.

She enquired sweetly, 'Where did you go to university?'

'Oxford and Harvard,' he said. 'With some time at the Sorbonne.' He added with a twist of his lips that revealed he'd guessed what she was thinking, 'My father valued education highly.'

'On Moraze as well as in his family?' she asked even more sweetly, then wished she'd remained silent.

Her urge to dig at his impervious facade was becoming reckless. And recklessness was something she didn't do.

In a level, unemphatic tone that managed to refute her snide insinuation, he said, 'Of course. Moraze has an excellent school system, and my father set up a scholarship scheme that offers promising students access to the best overseas universities.'

'Do you lose many to the lure of bigger, more sophisticated places?'

'We might, if they weren't bonded to come back here to work for five years; usually after that they're incorporated back into the fabric of our society. If not, they are then free to leave to pursue those goals.'

Lexie nodded, eyes widening as he got to his feet. Tall as she was, he towered over her so that she felt crowded. No, *dominated*, she thought, settling back into her chair and trying to look confident and at ease.

'I must go now,' he told her. 'If you need anything at all, tell Cari.'

An odd emptiness took her by surprise. 'I'm very grateful for everybody's kindness,' she said, and tried to sound her usual practical self as she went on, 'I assume I'll get a bill from the hospital—'

'No.'

'But I have travel insurance—'

'It isn't relevant,' he interrupted again, brows drawing together.

Head held so high it made her neck ache, Lexie got to her feet. Was he implying that he'd pay for it? Rich and powerful he might be, but she was an independent woman. 'Surely Moraze's health system bills travel insurance companies? In an island that depends on tourists—'

'We do not *depend* on tourists,' he said. 'We have an extremely good and progressive offshore banking system, and we have invested heavily in high-tech industries. Along with sugar, coffee and our gems, these are the pillars of our prosperity. Tourists are welcome, of course, but my government and I have taken note of the problems that come from too heavy a reliance on tourism.'

She would *not* let that aristocratic authority intimidate her. Steadily, each word bitten out, she said, 'Perhaps you would let me finish?'

A black eyebrow climbed, and his reply was delivered with a cool, autocratic politeness that reminded her he was almost a king. 'Of course. My apologies.'

'I pay my own way,' she said with brittle emphasis. 'And I pay my insurance company to cover me while I'm travelling.'

He measured her with one of those penetrating green surveys, then shrugged dismissively. 'I will make sure someone deals with it. I suggest that for the rest of today you take things quietly. There is a pool here, if you wish to swim, although it would be sensible not to go into the water until tomorrow.'

Lexie fought back a pang of humiliating disappointment, because that didn't sound as though he was coming back to the castle. She said with what she hoped was some dignity, 'Thank you very much for everything you've done.'

'It is my pleasure,' he said formally with a half bow, before turning on his heel to stride away.

Very much the man in control, she thought, subsiding back into the chair.

Very much the ruler of his own kingdom.

But why had he been so kind? If it *was* kindness that had persuaded him to bring her here to convalesce.

What else could it be? She gazed around at vivid flowers soaking up the sun, her gaze following a bird bright as a mobile bloom that darted from one heavily laden bush to another.

Uneasily she wondered if the kiss had had anything to do with his consideration. No; he'd given no indication that he even remembered that wild embrace.

Perhaps he was so accustomed to kissing women he'd forgotten. It had almost certainly been a whim, put behind him once he'd realised she didn't know much about kissing.

This holiday had seemed such a good idea; the chance to decide once and for all whether she and Felipe had a future together.

Now she wished she'd flown straight back home to New Zealand. Felipe's attempt to pressure her into his bed had convinced her she definitely didn't want any sort

of future with him, and meeting Rafiq had stirred something dark and disturbing in her, making her yearn for
some unknowable, unattainable goal.

Therese Fanchette said, 'You asked for a check to be kept
on Count Felipe Gastano.'

Not a muscle moved in her ruler's face, but she felt the
chill from across the big desk.

Eyes chips of green ice, Rafiq rapped out, 'So?'

'Information has come in about the Interpol operation.'

Rafiq's voice gave away nothing of the cold anger
biting into him. 'Is he aware of what's happening?'

'Not so far, as far as we can tell. His emails have been
intercepted, of course. There has been nothing to suggest
that anyone in his organisation has yet discovered our
plans.'

Rafiq dampened down his spurt of triumph. 'We need a
couple of days. Has he tried to contact M'selle Considine?'

'So far he has made several telephone calls to the castle.
Your people have said she is still resting.'

'It is strange that he knew I was involved in her rescue,
yet he has made no attempt to contact me.'

Therese Fanchette was one of the few people who knew
the reason for Rafiq's caution. She frowned, and said
slowly, 'Which leads one to suppose that he wants to keep
out of your way. One of Gastano's closest associates is
convinced that he plans to marry M'selle Considine.'

Rafiq's head came up and he stared at her. 'Is this good
information?' he demanded. 'Not just gossip?'

'I don't deal in gossip; this is as good as it gets. The
source mentioned that the date had been set. Has M'selle
Considine said anything about that? Or about Gastano?'

'Nothing,' he said briefly. 'Continue keeping him under observation. I want to know exactly what he is doing, where he goes, who he sees, and I want to make sure that he is unable to contact M'selle Considine for at least another couple of days.'

Therese inclined her head. 'Her phone calls and email are being monitored, as you requested. If he tries to contact her we will know immediately.' After a slight pause she said, 'With respect, sir, I still think it would be better to let them communicate with each other and see what we can learn.'

'I don't.'

She gave him what he called her grandmother's look, and his mouth quirked, his expression lightening. 'I know how you feel,' he admitted. 'I rarely have hunches, but something tells me to keep her under wraps for the present. If it achieves nothing else, the knowledge that his prospective bride is my guest and incommunicado should keep his mind off his overseas affairs.'

With a reluctant smile, Therese said, 'So far your hunches have been one-hundred-per-cent accurate, so I'd be stupid not to accept this one.'

'I realise it's likely to make things more difficult for you.' After another speaking look from her, his smile widened. 'But I'm sure you'll cope.'

When he was alone again he sat back at his desk and stared at the gold pen in front of him.

One part of him was icily furious that Gastano had dared set foot on Moraze, the other was bleakly satisfied—because now the count was in unfamiliar territory where the rules were different.

Greed bolstered by overconfidence often led to

mistakes, Rafiq thought with ruthless pragmatism. And coming to Moraze was the first mistake Gastano had made in a long time.

Rafiq got to his feet and walked over to the window, glancing up for a moment at the rampant stallion on the wall of his office, the badge of his house and the symbol of his family's rule. Everything he did was for Moraze's welfare.

So, was Lexie what she seemed to be, the complaisant lover of a high-flying criminal, in line to be his wife?

Or was she an innocent dupe, rather charming in her lack of sophistication?

If she wasn't a partner in Gastano's schemes, discovering the true nature of her lover could hurt her. But Rafiq knew he couldn't afford to be squeamish; he needed an edge over Gastano, and if the man planned to marry her this could be it.

Had Lexie been an innocent when she'd met the count?

A surge of lethal fury took Rafiq completely by surprise. Implacably, he fought it back, forcing himself to think analytically. It seemed unlikely. She'd spent years studying to be a vet, and, although universities were by no means hotbeds of vice, she was a very attractive woman with a swift, reckless sexual response that hinted at considerable experience.

Some of it gained in Gastano's bed, he reminded himself ruthlessly.

The memory of the kiss they'd exchanged still had the power to arouse Rafiq. What had been a rather sardonic whim on his part had changed the instant his lips met hers. She'd been vividly, tantalisingly passionate, and he'd lost himself in her open sensuality.

That kiss had been surprisingly hard to break away from—and even harder to forget.

His household offices were in the old citadel, built on a spur of volcanic rock that overtopped the city by some hundred or so metres, so he had an excellent view of the business district. His gaze skimmed the glittering water of the port, and the bright trees that lined the business area, then beyond to the houses clinging to the surrounding hills.

Logically, dispassionately, he considered the situation, examining it from all angles until he finally came to a conclusion. It was a difficult one, but he had been trained to make difficult decisions, even ones that threatened to exact a personal cost.

As the sweet-scented tropical day drew to a close, Lexie felt so much better she thought quite seriously about heading back to the hotel. Common sense decided that tomorrow would probably be a better day. The maid had insisted she rest again before dinner, closing the shutters even while Lexie was trying to persuade her that she wasn't tired.

'The Emir says it is necessary,' Cari said firmly.

Rafiq the Emir. It suited him, Lexie thought with an odd little shiver.

To her astonishment she did sleep again, lulled by the distant thunder of the waves on the reef, waking to a feeling of lazy wellbeing, a kind of hopeful anticipation, as though something wonderful was in store, something she'd waited for without even realising it…

'Just watch yourself,' she said aloud.

But that rash eagerness persisted even after she'd got up, even though she knew Rafiq wasn't coming back.

Irritated by the wistful tone of her thoughts, she made an impatient gesture.

So she was attracted to him. Why should that startle her? Plenty of other women at the party had watched him from the corners of their eyes, avidly appreciating his superb male assets. Like this castle, her suite, her bathroom, he was straight out of a fairy tale—a ruler, strong, and more than a little intimidating.

He'd asked her if she liked the thought of taming a man.

Flushing, she went to brush her hair. The answer was still no, but it would be…exciting to discover whether *his* imperious control was unbreakable.

Meeting—being kissed by—Rafiq de Couteveille had summoned a hidden, shameful yearning.

To be beautiful.

There, she'd said it, but only in her mind. To rub in how completely ridiculous she was being, she forced the words through her lips: 'I'd like to be beautiful. I'd like him to look at me the way Marco looks at Jacoba. Even once would do.'

A swift, derisory glance at the mirror revealed why that would never happen. 'There's nothing *wrong* with you—you're just *ordinary*,' she said, pronouncing the word like a curse.

She stared more closely at her reflection, clinically cataloguing her assets.

Good skin, though it turned sallow if she didn't choose the right colours to wear.

Fine features, but without anything of Jacoba's witchery.

OK eyes, darkish blue, set off by black brows and long lashes.

Hair that was wavy and thick, boring brown with gold highlights in the sun.

And although she had quite a reasonable figure, she lacked any lush curves; slim and athletic was probably as good as it got.

Lexie curled her lip. All in all—*forgettable.*

And the kiss they'd shared had clearly meant so little to Rafiq he'd relegated it to some dark cupboard in his memory, never to be opened again.

Which was what *she* should do, she decided, ashamed by her neediness. It embarrassed her that the independence she'd taken so much for granted had crumbled at one touch from a man's practised mouth.

She was Lexie Sinclair, and she was a vet—a *good* vet—and she'd be a better one before she finished. Always she'd gratefully left the limelight to Jacoba and followed her own less-spectacular dreams. Being thrust into the Illyrian spotlight had shocked her, and awakened a difficult conscience within herself, one that forced her to do what she could to alleviate her father's bitter, brutal legacy. She was proud of what she'd achieved in her year in Illyria. But now it was over she craved privacy, and the chance to get on with the life she'd planned.

So how the heck had she ended up in a royal palace on an exotic island in the Indian Ocean, with the most handsome prince in the world as her reluctant host?

'Sheer chance. And you'll soon be out of here,' she told herself. 'Then you can forget about this interlude.'

But even as she turned away and dressed she knew she'd never forget Rafiq de Couteveille.

The tropical twilight was draping the hills in a hazy robe when she made her way down the stairs. At the bottom of the flight, a table stood with a huge vase of flowers, some completely alien to Lexie. Entranced by their colours and shapes, she stopped to admire them, but her attention was caught by a photograph beside the urn.

A girl—in her mid-teens perhaps, and clearly a close relative of Rafiq. Her bright, beautiful face was a softened version of his features.

From behind, Cari said, 'The Emir's sister.'

'I didn't know he had a sister,' Lexie said rapidly, warned by a note in the older woman's voice that something was amiss.

The maid looked sadly at the photograph. 'Her name was Hani. She is dead since two years,' she said. 'I will show you to the courtyard.'

'I know the way to it.'

'I think not. You sat with the Emir in the garden. This is different.'

Lexie followed her into an arcaded square, where a fountain played musically in a grassy lawn sectioned into quarters by gravel paths. Flowering shrubs were set out in patterns, the formal style tempered by luxuriant growth and the penetrating, languorous perfumes of the tropics. Along the wall that looked out over the sea was another arcade, deeply shadowed.

After telling the maid that she needed nothing, Lexie was left alone to watch the darkness come, surprised that it brought no coolness. Within minutes the sea was cloaked and the stars sprang out, forming their ancient patterns in the velvet sky.

An ache chilled her heart. How had that vital, laughing girl died? Straightening up, she turned to go back inside. Her skin tightened when she saw Rafiq walk out, and wildfire anticipation flared to life in her guarded heart.

This was what she'd been waiting for.

A faint tremor tempered her first undisciplined emotion when Rafiq came towards her—tall, powerfully built and compelling as a panther. He looked austere, as harshly forbidding as that long-ago desert sheikh who'd lost his favourite daughter to a French exile.

No words formed in her brain; silent, except for the thudding of her heartbeat in her ears, she watched him approach and wished she'd worn something more sophisticated than trousers and a shirt.

Because she felt stupid just standing there and staring, she tried for a smile, holding it pinned to her lips for a few seconds too long to be natural.

He stopped a few feet away and treated her to another trademark survey, swift and unwavering, his gaze ranging across her face.

One foolish hand started to move in an instinctive attempt to shield herself. Hastily she controlled the betraying gesture, straightening her arm.

'Have you a headache?' he demanded sharply, crossing the intervening space in three long strides.

'No.'

But he'd already taken her chin in his hand and was examining her face carefully, running his fingers through the hair at her temple where her own hand had strayed. Something sparked in the dark green eyes, and Lexie felt herself melting, her bones turning heavy and lax, a tide of honeyed sensation stirring inside her.

In a quick, panicked voice, she said, 'I'm perfectly all right. My head didn't get hurt.' Her neck still spasmed when she turned it incautiously, but apart from that she felt remarkably fit.

He let her go and stepped back, his mouth held in an uncompromising line. 'So I see. Cari tells me you have slept again. You look better.'

'I do, thank you.' Self-consciously she cleared her throat because something had caught in it, turning her normally clear tones husky.

'Good. Come and sit down. Would you like something to drink?' When she hesitated, he smiled and added, 'Without alcohol, if you prefer that.'

'It sounds perfect.' She tried to hide a treacherous surge of dizziness at that killer smile.

Something had changed, she thought as he took her elbow in an automatic gesture. She didn't exactly know what, but some instinct sensed a softening—well, no, an awareness—in him that hadn't been there before in spite of his consideration for her.

Rafiq sat her down, silently appreciating her smooth, lithe grace as she sank into the comfortable chair he held.

'This courtyard was built by one of my ancestors for his bride,' he told her when Lexie looked around with a soft sigh of pleasure. She was very tactile, responding immediately to beauty. Would she be as open and ardent when she made love?

Ruthlessly he disciplined his unruly mind. 'She was from the south of Spain, and he wanted to give her something that would remind her of home, so he built her a serenity garden, something like the one in the Alhambra. She loved it, as did later wives.'

'So this place has been a home for a long time?'

He nodded. 'After the corsairs were defeated, yes, it

became the residence of the oldest son. Until a hundred years or so ago, the actual ruler still lived in the citadel above the capital.'

He handed her a glass of juice, cool and refreshing. 'I hope you enjoy this. It's mostly lime juice, but there is some papaya there, and a local herb that's supposed to heal bruises.'

'It's delicious,' she said after a tentative sip. 'That citadel looks pretty grim. I doubt if the wives of the heirs ever wanted to leave this lovely place for it.'

Stepping back, Rafiq tore his gaze from her lips and fought back a surge of desire. He'd watched hundreds of women drink a variety of liquids, and none of them had ever affected him like this woman.

Masking his intense physical reaction with cool detachment, he answered, 'It was largely rebuilt in the nineteenth century, and is now used as offices for my household.'

He looked down, noting her interested expression, and wondered angrily what it was about her that bypassed the strictures of his brain and homed straight onto his groin. Taken feature by feature, she wasn't even beautiful. Superb skin enlivened by smoky-blue eyes and a mouth that more than lived up to its sensual promise did make her alluring. But he'd made love to some of the world's most beautiful women without feeling anything like this primitive desire to possess that gripped him whenever he saw Lexie Sinclair.

CHAPTER FIVE

RAFIQ enquired, 'You are interested in history?'

Lexie gave a rueful little smile, wondering what was going on behind the angular mask of his features. 'Because we're such a young country, most New Zealanders are impressed by anything that's more than a couple of hundred years old.'

'Moraze has a history stretching back a couple of thousand years, possibly even longer,' he told her. 'Certainly, the Arabs knew of its existence well before the end of the first millennium—its name is from the Arabic, meaning East Island, because it lies east of Zanzibar.'

East of Zanzibar—oh, the phrase had magic, she thought dreamily. *Anything* could happen east of Zanzibar. You could meet an excitingly dangerous man and discover things about yourself that shocked you.

You could even find your ultimate soul mate…

Hastily she dragged herself back to reality. 'I'm surprised they didn't exploit the fire-diamonds. Surely any trader worth his salt would have realised how incredibly valuable they were?'

Thick, black lashes covered Rafiq's hard eyes for a

second before he shrugged. 'Before they are cut they look like mere pebbles, so they weren't discovered until a hundred years or so after the first de Couteveille arrived. If you're interested, there are ruins of unknown origin in the hills of the escarpment further to the north.'

'Really?'

'When you're fully recovered I will take you there,' he said casually.

A feverish thrill tightened Lexie's skin. He was watching her, and as their eyes met he smiled, a slow movement of his mouth that sent even more chills of excitement through her. He sounded as though he was looking forward to the promised excursion as much as she was.

Help! Thoughts chased through her head in tumultuous distraction. She took a swift breath and said sedately, 'How very intriguing. Does anyone have any theory on who built them?'

'Theories abound,' he informed her dryly. 'Some say they are the original Atlantis, some that they were made by the Trojans when they fled Troy, some that the people who built them came from China.'

'Are they being excavated?'

'Yes.'

He told her about the ruins and the museum, and university teams that had combined to excavate them. He astonished her with tales of the furious war of words that had broken out between two extremely opinionated archaeologists, a battle fought through the media, until finally Rafiq had threatened to ban both of them from ever coming to Moraze again.

'It seems incongruous for people whose profession is

to find the truth to be so hidebound and one-eyed,' Lexie said thoughtfully.

'Egos often get in the way of the truth. Egos and greed.'

The words fell into the scented air, flat and cold and uncompromising, so much at variance with the soft hushing of the water in the fountain and the overarching infinity of the sable sky above that Lexie shivered. 'Greed? Surely archaeologists don't profit financially from their discoveries?'

'Profit need not be financial. An interesting set of ruins well-excavated will build a reputation. Greed for the possible rewards of a big discovery can override common sense, and sometimes even lead to destructive actions.'

It sounded like a warning—one directed at her.

Did he know about her father? Greed and ego had led him to do monstrous things.

Shaken by the nausea that always affected her when she thought of the man who had sired her, Lexie sipped more of the delicious juice and said colourlessly, 'I suppose you're right.'

Dismissing the subject, Rafiq got to his feet. 'Are you ready for dinner?'

'Yes, thank you.' But she stood too fast; the abrupt movement sent a jab of pain through her neck, making her clamp her lips together.

She didn't think he'd noticed, but it took him only a second to reach her, his hands gripping her shoulders from behind as he asked, 'What is it? What's the matter? This is the second time you've almost fainted.'

'I didn't.' Her voice sounded thin and far away, so she swallowed and tried again. 'I must have twisted my neck in the accident. It's fine, but every now and then the muscles remind me of it. It's nothing.'

His grasp eased, but he didn't let her go, still so close that she could discern his subtle, potent male scent.

'Perhaps this will help,' he said quietly, his thumbs moving in slow circles on the nape of her neck.

Sensuous little chills raced down her spine. Lexie closed her eyes, but that made her pulse rate soar even higher; an odd weakness in her bones threatened her with an undignified collapse. Resisting the temptation to lean back, she forced her eyes open and stared belligerently ahead, blinking to clear the dreamy haze from her sight.

Break it up right now, caution warned. She said curtly, 'I'm perfectly all right, thank you.'

'Are you?' A raw note in the words caught her attention as he turned her to face him.

She looked up into an angular visage, all hard lines and intensity. What she saw there drove every thought into oblivion.

Green eyes blazing, he bent his head. 'You don't look *all right*. Shall I carry you to your room?'

'No!' Sheer panic raised her voice.

Panic—and a wild response that blazed up from nowhere, licking through her like the best brandy, burning away inhibitions and restraint in a conflagration of need.

'Your eyes give your words the lie.' He dropped his narrowed gaze to her mouth. 'And that delicious mouth makes promises I want to collect on.'

Struggling for control, she shook her head.

'Say it,' he said in a harsh voice. 'Tell me you don't want me as much as I want you.'

Lexie's breath stopped in her throat. Her muscles locked as she met his gleaming gaze with a challenge she couldn't hide.

'Say no—or take the consequences.' This time he spoke more gently.

Wordlessly she lifted a hand to his cheek.

Half smiling, he teased her with kisses on the corners of her willing mouth. An inarticulate little sound from her made him smile, but in answer to her wordless plea he deepened the kiss, and his arms clamped her against the lean strength of his body.

The tension between them was now revealed for what it was—a fierce sexual charge that hungered for this, for more…

Rafiq lifted his head to tilt hers back, so that he could kiss the length of her throat, stopping only a fraction above the neckline of the prim silk shirt she'd bought half a world away in Illyria.

Lexie's heart literally jumped; she was sure she felt it move in her breast, then settle back into place before he said against her skin, 'You have the mouth of a siren.'

His faint accent intensified so that he sounded exotic—almost barbaric. 'And you kiss like one. Where did you learn that?'

'I don't—I don't think you *learn* to kiss,' she parried breathlessly, aware only that she couldn't let him see how much that final caress had shattered her once-safe world.

One black brow arched. 'Perhaps not,' he drawled.

And he kissed her again, mercilessly stoking the craving that ate into her, a wild, primal longing for union, a desire that burned hotter and even hotter until she was aching, her body poised and eager, her mind clouded as though with drugs.

Alarm bells rang. When he lifted his head and let his gaze slide downwards, she realised that her inner turbulence was physically revealed; her breasts had peaked, demanding a satisfaction only Rafiq could give her.

Shocked, she pulled back. For a second she thought he was going to keep her in his arms by force, but then he gave a twisted, rather sardonic smile and let her go.

'No,' he stated rather than asked.

'Dinner must be ready.' Although her voice was hoarse and uneven, she met his gaze steadily, without flinching.

His laughter held no amusement. 'Indeed, and one should never keep the servants waiting. This way.'

He extended his arm. After a moment's hesitation Lexie laid her fingertips on it, feeling the slow flex of his muscle beneath them with a voluptuous thrill—half forbidden desire, half fear.

This was *dangerous*, she warned herself silently as they walked across the great hall.

'You are afraid of me?' His tone was aloof, at odds with the penetrating look he sent her.

'No,' she said rapidly. 'Of course not.'

The person she was terrified of was herself. She appeared to have no resistance to Rafiq's particular brand of potent masculinity, and her abandon startled and dismayed her.

Stiffly, her voice as brittle as her tight-strung body, she said, 'I don't normally make a habit of kissing near strangers like—like that.' The last few words rushed out. Aware that she'd probably revealed more than she wanted him to know, she straightened her shoulders and stared straight ahead.

'I guessed as much.'

His worldliness shattered what remained of her composure. Was he insinuating that she was transparently inexperienced?

Well, she was, she thought stoutly, and what did it matter whether her untutored response to his kisses had told him so?

He finished with forbidding emphasis, 'And you need not worry—I do not force women.'

'I… Well, I'm sure you don't,' she said warily, then stopped when she saw where he was leading her. 'Oh—oh! Oh, how *lovely*.'

They'd gone up one floor and through a small salon that opened out into air lit by lamps, their warm glow illuminating a wide, stone terrace, and a row of arches on the seaward side that were latticed with stone delicately carved into flowers and leaves. Shrubs and trees cooled the terrace and shielded it from prying eyes. At one end a lily-starred pool surrounded a roofed pavilion, connected to the terrace by a stone bridge. Behind floating, gauzy drapes, Lexie discerned the outlines of furniture.

'Another whim of yet another besotted ancestor,' Rafiq explained with a touch of irony. 'He rescued his wife from a corsair ship; she loved to swim, and he loved to join her, so he built this pool and made sure it couldn't be overlooked.'

The kisses they'd exchanged suddenly loomed very large in Lexie's mind. Was he indicating…?

A sideways glance at his face banished that vagrant thought. He wasn't even looking at her, and it was impossible to read anything from his expression.

Rafiq looked down and caught her watching him. His lashes drooped, and she asked too hastily, 'Why was she on a corsair ship? Was she a pirate too?'

He stopped by the bridge. 'She was the daughter of the British governor of a West Indian island, snatched for ransom, but the captain found her appealing enough to keep her. When the Caribbean got too hot for him, he fled to the Indian Ocean. She waited until they approached Moraze, intent as they were on plunder, then managed to wound her abductor severely enough to escape and swim ashore.'

Startled, Lexie looked up from her contemplation of the water lilies. They weren't growing in the pool, as she'd first thought, but had been cut and floated on the water, a medley of white and palest yellow. Their scent teased her nostrils. 'She must have been a very resourceful woman.'

Her companion showed his teeth in a smile that held more than a hint of ruthlessness. 'I come from a long line of people who did what they had to do to survive,' he said evenly. 'Some weren't particularly scrupulous, or even likeable; some embraced revenge without compunction if it served their plans. She hated her captor.'

A little shiver snaked down Lexie's backbone, and memories of her father's actions clouded her eyes. 'Very few people can claim to have only saints in their lineage.'

He smiled cynically. 'Agreed.'

'So what happened to the governor's daughter after she swam to Moraze?'

'My ancestor found her hiding on shore. She told him of the corsair's plans, and with his men he captured the ship, killing the man who'd abducted her. Apparently she and my ancestor quarrelled furiously for several months, then astonished everyone by marrying.' This time Rafiq's smile showed real amusement. 'They had a long and happy life together, but they were not a peaceful couple.'

'I'm glad she found happiness after such an ordeal,' Lexie said. 'As for peace, well, some people find peace boring.'

'Are you one of them?' he asked, indicating that they should cross the bridge.

Lexie frowned. It sounded like a throwaway question, yet somehow she sensed a thread of intention, of significance, in his words that made her feel uneasy and dangerously vulnerable. Was he exploring her personality, or just keeping the conversation alive?

Almost certainly the latter, common sense told her, and yet...

Because the silence threatened to last too long, she set out briskly across the bridge. 'As a vet I don't like too much excitement—it tends to involve going out in the middle of the night in filthy weather to deal with sick, very expensive animals and their frantic owners! But I certainly enjoy variety.'

There, that was innocuous enough, surely? She didn't want to get into anything heavy here. Although they'd kissed—and he'd seemed to enjoy those kisses—she wasn't going to let herself fall into the trap of believing they'd meant anything more to him than the superficial response of a virile man to a woman of the right age to mate.

A woman whose instant arousal, she thought with a burning shame, must make it obvious she found him irresistible.

But then, he'd be used to that response—it probably happened in every female who set eyes on him.

And to quench the flickering embers of desire she'd better stop this train of thought right now. So she asked, 'What about you?'

'I enjoy moments of peace,' Rafiq said, his tone giving nothing away. 'But I think a life of unalloyed tranquillity and harmony could become tedious after a while. I relish a challenge.'

'Oh, so do I,' she responded, and changed the subject abruptly. 'The water lilies here must be different from the ones at home. Ours fold up at dusk.'

'So do ours.' He smiled. 'I believe the petals of these ones are held in place by candle wax. It is a local tradition.'

A few steps brought them to the pavilion, where Rafiq held the drapes back with a lean hand. 'Do you play chess?'

'Badly,' she replied, walking into the airy space and looking around. 'I don't think I'd be even the mildest challenge to anyone who can think more than two moves ahead.'

But several hours later, after they'd eaten, she was sitting on the edge of her chair and glowering at an elaborate chessboard, her mind working frantically.

Rafiq said evenly, 'You lied.'

Her head came up, and she met his half-closed green eyes with a flash of fire. 'I don't lie.'

'You said you were no challenge.' His voice was amused.

'You're winning,' she pointed out. 'In fact, I can't see how I'm going to get out of this situation.'

He lifted his brows. 'If you want to know—'

'No! Give me another few minutes to see if I can do it.'

His quick grin—so unlike his usual air of sophisticated forcefulness that it startled her—was quickly controlled. 'Go ahead,' he invited.

Frowning, Lexie puzzled over the board, saw what seemed to be the perfect move, and almost made it—until further intense thought revealed it would involve a check to her king a few moves further on.

Rafiq had a poker player's face; not a single emotion escaped his control. She was acutely, violently aware of him at his ease in the cane chair, long limbs relaxed, the light from a dozen soft lamps highlighting the arrogant sweep of cheekbones, the tough jawline and the hooded green of his eyes.

Lexie's breath caught in her throat. Behind him she could see several elegant loungers, and a day bed—a sinful thing, more than big enough to hold two people during the hours of a lazy tropical siesta. A puff of breeze smoothed over her skin, sensitising it...

Every coherent thought died a swift and unappreciated death, drowned by a sensuous recklessness. *I want you*, she thought, the need so violent she wondered for a panicky second if she'd actually said it.

Colour burned her cheeks. She had to get out of there, away from this man—away from this love nest with its scented flowers and gentle lamplight. Abruptly she said, 'Do you mind if I call it a day? I'll concede if you'll tell me how to get out of this.'

One black brow climbed, but he showed her.

As they blocked out the moves, he said in a casual voice, 'In two days' time I will be attending a special function— the opening ceremony for another hotel, but this time the celebrations are for those who worked on the building, and those who will work in it. A people's party, much less formal than the affair you attended the other night. If you feel up to it, would you like to come with me?'

Completely taken aback, she flushed again, searching for words. 'I feel fine, but I don't want to intrude... I'll be quite happy here, you know.'

His all-too-potent smile sent erotic little shivers through

her. 'There will be music and dancing and excellent food, and very few speeches.'

Torn, Lexie hesitated. Being with Rafiq was starting to mean far too much. A sensible woman would find some good excuse to refuse.

Deciding that being sensible was vastly overrated, she strove for some of his confidence. 'I'd love to come. It sounds like great fun.'

'I hope so.'

Rafiq wondered what was going on behind that serene face. She didn't realise that she was actually a prisoner in the castle; he hoped she never would.

Not for the first time he wondered how an intelligent, accomplished woman like her had been duped by Gastano. Was she bored with the man? She hadn't tried to contact the count, and certainly she'd shown no signs of missing him.

Which could mean that to her the relationship was as superficial as Gastano's charm.

It seemed likely. Rafiq's mind ranged back to the first time they'd met; she'd been offhand with the count, and in spite of Gastano's presence she'd been acutely aware of Rafiq.

As physically aware as he'd been of her.

Lust at first sight, he thought, controlling a cold, humourless smile. His jaw hardened as Lexie began to pack away the chessmen in their carved box.

Did she know Gastano intended marriage? It didn't seem likely. Or was this her way of showing Gastano that she'd wanted no more than an affair with him?

If so, she had no understanding of her lover. Her family connections would be worth more than gold to the count.

As her husband, he'd have entrée into a milieu he'd long coveted—the charmed world of royal power and influence.

The count would be furious if he thought the woman he'd targeted as a ticket to respectability and even greater power was slipping through his fingers.

And furious men made mistakes.

Gastano had already tried to establish contact with Lexie. Rafiq recalled Gastano's email note, written in a tone he probably intended to be disarming, but with enough innuendo to summon a shockingly forthright and very territorial response from Rafiq. And although he couldn't find a logical reason for it, he still felt strongly that hiding her away from Gastano was the only way to keep her safe.

Because of Hani? He dismissed that thought. His sister had been naïve; Lexie was not. Even if she had been when she met Gastano, two months as his mistress would have put paid to any innocence.

The question Rafiq couldn't ask nagged at him. Had she responded to Gastano with the same wildfire passion she'd revealed in his own arms?

The thought made his fists clench. Watching the way the golden lamplight shifted and shimmered across her bent head as she carefully sorted the chessmen, Rafiq wondered again if his objectivity was being hijacked by his response to her. Those smoky blue eyes, half-hidden by her long, black lashes, might mask her thoughts, but nothing could disguise that softly sensuous mouth.

His gaze hardened as Lexie slid the queens into place, capable fingers moving swiftly, her lashes casting shadowy fans on her exquisite skin.

Lexie looked up to find her host's dark eyes on her, intent and speculative, as though trying to see into her soul. Her nerves sparked and colour heated her cheeks.

'You look tired,' he said quietly. 'How is your neck?'

Her colour deepened. 'It's fine, thank you. It just catches me now and then.'

She took her time about closing the case that held the chess set, fiddling with the catch until she regained some composure. But although her skin was cool once more, the fire inside her still burned with a fierce, hungry flame.

Getting to her feet, she said a little shortly, 'It's been a lovely evening. Thank you.'

He rose with her, looking down from his considerably superior height with a smile that didn't reach his eyes. They walked in silence across the bridge and back through the castle.

Lexie wished she could be as controlled. His nearness was delicious torture. She both longed for the door of her room and resented its imminence, torn between this dangerously addictive arousal and the knowledge that the chemistry between them meant nothing more than uncomplicated, old-fashioned animal magnetism.

Looked at from a biological point of view, she thought, trying hard to be dispassionate and scientific, the volatile attraction pounding through her bloodstream and alerting every cell in her body was a natural urge stimulated by hormones that somehow knew she and Rafiq would make splendid children together.

Something deep inside her melted.

Ruthlessly she told herself it didn't mean she was in love with him. He certainly wasn't in love with her. It was simply a matter of genes, the need to perpetuate the species—all the things she'd learned in her long and expensive university training.

And although her response to him was a fiery torment, it didn't really mean much. Worldwide, there were probably millions of men she could feel this way about.

She'd just never met one before.

Anyway, when she married she wanted what Jacoba had—a man who adored her and accepted her as his equal in every way.

Not someone who saw her simply as a sexual partner.

Rafiq's voice broke in on her ragged thoughts as they reached the door of her room. 'That is an interesting expression.'

She stiffened, her brain searching for something innocuous to say. Lamely—and too quickly—she said, 'I was thinking about a biological… Ah, about biology.'

His lips curved in a wry, humourless smile, and his eyes were darkly shaded. 'So was I.' The last word was spoken against her eager, expectant mouth.

His previous kisses had been explorations, she thought dimly; this one wasn't. He knew what she wanted, and when she gave a muffled groan and surrendered, he gathered her even closer so that she could feel his physical reaction—the electric intensity of his desire, the erotic difference between her female softness and his male power.

A rush of adrenalin sharpened her senses as her body sprang into exhilarating life. Shivering with delight, she forgot everything but the sheer physical magic of his embrace and her mindless, primal response. His body heat, the strength of his hands on her, the faint, intrinsic scent of him, the tactile excitement of his skin beneath her seeking fingers—all combined to add sensual fuel to that inner fire burning away inhibitions and caution.

CHAPTER SIX

RAFIQ loosened his arms and rested his cheek on the top of Lexie's head, gently rocking her in his arms while she came back to earth.

'It is too soon,' he said, his voice oddly harsh. 'And although you are like wildfire in my arms, there are smudges under those beautiful eyes, and I think you are trying to stifle a yawn in my shoulder. Good night, Lexie. Sleep well. Tomorrow I will take you on the trip that was cut short by the accident.'

She might see something of the famed wild horses of Moraze. Lexie should have been delighted. To her shock and dismay, all she could summon was mild enthusiasm. Stifling a small sound of protest, she composed her expression into serenity and eased back, feeling foolishly bereft when he let her go with insulting ease.

'I'll look forward to that.' Oh Lord; her voice was breathy and soft, as though she were mimicking Marilyn Monroe!

Without meeting his eyes, she directed a swift, shaken smile at him and turned into her room, nerves jumping when she closed the door. She leaned back against the carved wood, striving to force strength into her lax bones.

This whole situation was too dangerous. She shouldn't have allowed those passionate moments in his arms, moments charged with a carnal magic that still ached through her.

Allowed them? She'd welcomed them, surrendered to them, wallowed in the erotic excitement of them, until in the end she'd had no defences left. The intensity of her emotions, the sensations Rafiq made her feel, scared her. When he touched her she lost herself, became someone different, an alien person with no shame and no control.

Lexie wrenched herself upright and walked across to a window, staring out across the lagoon to the white line of the reef.

Slowly she dragged air into her lungs. These bewildering days on Moraze were teaching her that she wasn't capable of an easy relationship with lots of lust followed by a cheerful goodbye once it was sated.

'Not my style,' she said a little bitterly to the silent room. Certainly not with Rafiq...

But at least she'd learned one thing about him: he didn't want just casual sex either. Because he could have had her right there and then, and he'd known it, yet he'd pulled back.

She set her jaw. Because her resistance was so easily breached, there must be no more of this perilous intimacy. After tomorrow she'd leave the castle. And she'd make it clear she wasn't in the market for, well, anything. He wouldn't press her; Rafiq de Couteveille was a sophisticated man, and there were plenty of sophisticated, experienced women who'd be more than happy to satisfy his urges.

And that sharp stab of emotion was *not* jealousy, or—worse still—anguish at the thought!

'There!' Rafiq pointed over her shoulder, his voice urgent. 'Can you see them?'

'Yes.' Thrilled, Lexie lifted the binoculars he'd lent her and examined the small herd.

Not at all spooked by the vehicle, the horses lifted their heads and serenely surveyed them. A couple of skittish youngsters danced sideways, their coats gleaming in the tropical sun, only to subside and snatch another mouthful of grass. The stallion, master of his harem, clearly realised that no harm would come to them from this particular vehicle. Although he kept a watchful eye on them, his stance showed his trust. Even the wise old mare that led the herd had already dropped her head to graze again.

Lexie stole another glance at the arrogant line of Rafiq's profile as he watched the herd. The angular lines of his face intent yet relaxed, he looked as though the sight of the herd satisfied a hunger in his soul. Her heartbeat picked up speed. How would she feel if he ever gazed at her like that?

Angry with herself at such futile longing, she lifted the binoculars to her eyes again. 'How long have they been on Moraze?'

'The bride of the first de Couteveille brought some of her father's horses with her. They were set free up here, and here they've flourished ever since.'

Like the de Couteveilles, she thought. She said on a sigh, 'I'll always remember this day. Thank you so much.'

'It has been my pleasure,' he said calmly, and set the four-wheel drive in motion. As they started on the winding descent to the fertile lowlands, he asked, 'Which did you enjoy most—the jungle animals in the mountains, or the horses?'

She laughed. 'That's an unfair question, but I was fascinated by the jungle animals, and can't help wondering how on earth their ancestors got here.'

'Biologists are working on their provenance,' he told her. Without any change in tone he went on, 'So you liked the horses better?'

Surprised at his perception, she admitted, 'Yes. They're so wild and free, and so lovely. I suppose I envy them.'

'Perhaps we all do.' He sent her a glance that set her toes tingling. 'But you have independence. Or are you planning to give it up?'

Startled, she said quickly, 'No.'

His glance sharpened before he returned it to the road ahead. 'What appeals to you so much about the thought of freedom?'

'Surely it's everyone's desire?' She looked ahead to the vehicle that accompanied them, driven by a bodyguard with another by his side. Living like that would stifle her. How did Rafiq stand it?

'Most people seem content to settle into comfortable servitude,' he observed.

'Perhaps. And perhaps they're happier than those who long for freedom.' She looked up. 'Are you content with your chains?'

'Tell me what you think to be my chains.'

'Well, you're forced to live as the ruler of Moraze. Don't you ever have the urge to break free?'

His gaze flicked across her face, then returned to the road ahead. 'Sometimes,' he said, shrugging. 'And you? What chains hold you?'

Lexie bit her lip. Like him, servitude to her forebears, but she wasn't going to tell him about her father. 'Oh, nothing really,' she said lamely, wishing she hadn't embarked on this.

She stared around, then said, 'Oh! I recognise this place—it's where we crashed!' Frowning, she leaned forward to examine the road and the grassy bank as they passed the spot. 'I wonder why I didn't see the animal that ran out in front of us.'

'It's possible you did see it, but because of the shock you don't remember,' Rafiq said coolly. 'The driver has recovered completely, by the way.'

'I still feel guilty because I didn't go to see her,' Lexie said without thinking.

He shrugged. 'You have high standards of behaviour. She did not expect it.'

Something in his tone made her say crisply, 'Simple courtesy isn't exactly a high standard.' And without finesse she steered the conversation in another direction. 'Tell me, what should I wear to the hotel party? I don't know the sort of thing that would be appropriate.'

He sent her another enigmatic glance, almost as though she'd surprised him. 'The dress you wore the night we met would be perfect.'

The flame-shot silk Jacoba had bought for her? Lexie loved that dress, and not just because the colour brought out a richness in her hair, and gave her skin a glow it didn't normally have. In it she felt like someone else—a different, bolder, more confident person.

Torn between a desire to look her best and a cowardly caution, she hesitated, fixing her gaze on the scenery as Rafiq steered the vehicle around a set of hairpin bends.

When they'd been safely and skilfully negotiated, she asked, 'Are you sure?'

'I am,' he said, and smiled, a slow, amused curl of his beautiful mouth that sent excitement flickering through her. 'Colour is important here,' he went on. 'It seems to be a tropical thing. In cooler climates, people wear more subdued hues.'

'Possibly because we have paler colouring, and vivid shades tend to wash us out.'

'But not you,' he told her with the confidence of a man who saw nothing unusual in discussing clothes with a woman.

The crisp note of challenge in his tone brought up her chin. 'Then I'll wear the dress.'

Only to stop there, because she didn't know what to say next.

Although he didn't seem to be flirting with her, there was definitely an appreciative glint in the greenstone gaze when it skimmed her face before returning to the road.

'Whatever you wear you will look good,' he said almost dismissively as he guided the vehicle around another hairpin bend.

Lexie didn't know whether it was a compliment or a sop to her rare lack of confidence.

'Thank you,' she said spiritedly, wishing she'd dated more often, even indulged in a couple of affairs. Surely experience would have given her some idea of how to deal with him?

Probably not, she thought with a touch of cynicism, watching the trees flash by—a coastal forest sparser than the jungle. Rafiq de Couteville, ruler of Moraze, was no ordinary man.

'The jungle reminded me of New Zealand,' she said absently. 'Those massive trees with their huge trunks reaching for the sky, each notch and fork filled with epiphytes—just like home!'

'Rain forest looks similar the world over. I've seen photographs of New Zealand trees; I was most impressed with the size and the majesty—the authority—of those huge trees that grow in the north. Kauri, are they not?'

'Yes. Northern New Zealand's iconic tree, along with the coastal pohutukawa, and true lords of the bush.'

She looked away again, longing to be safely back home, away from all this perilous beauty, the constant sensation of being watched and somehow under siege.

Sheer imagination, of course. And although she was out of her depth with Rafiq she wasn't green enough to take his embraces seriously, no matter how powerfully she was affected by them.

Yes, he'd been kind—well, taking her into his home after the accident was more than simple kindness—but that didn't mean anything. He'd probably have been just as considerate—without the kisses!—if she'd been fifty and grey-haired.

The road straightened once they reached the fertile plains, rich with sugar cane plantations and farms where flowers grew in ribbons and rainbows of saturated colour—seductive, scented orchids, the polished brilliance of anthuriums, and the erect, surreal stems of ginger in all their bold, vibrant hues.

Lexie let out her breath on a soft sigh. 'This is so beautiful.'

'Indeed,' he said calmly, and sent her another sideways glance. 'Are you tired? There is a place you might like to see a little farther on.'

'I feel fine.' An understatement if ever there was one; her mind and senses were at full stretch, intensely stimulated by his potent, compelling presence.

He touched a button and spoke in the local language to the car in front. A few moments later he slowed the car, took a sharp intersection and headed up into the mountains again through jungle that got more and more dense as they climbed.

'We are going to a lake that occupies an extinct volcanic crater,' he told her. 'The islanders believe it is the home of a particularly beautiful but extremely dangerous fairy, who has been known to amuse herself by seducing young men and then sending them away. They become afflicted with love for her, and drown as they try to swim back to her arms.'

Lexie repressed an odd little shiver to ask lightly, 'And does this happen often?'

He sent her an amused glance. 'Not within living memory, but that may be because most young men are careful not to go there until they are married. She isn't interested in married men, apparently.'

'You're not afraid?' she asked with a teasing smile, then wished she hadn't.

His response was sardonic. 'Not a bit,' he said coolly. 'I have yet to meet a woman I'd drown for.'

Her heart clamped tight. He was warning her off—why?

Last night when he'd stopped their lovemaking she'd been impressed because she'd thought it meant he didn't want just sex from her. Had she misread his consideration?

Perhaps his blunt statement of a moment ago was intended to convey that he didn't plan a serious relationship.

Was there a sophisticated way to tell him flatly that she

wasn't foolish enough—even in her dreams—to have hoped for that…?

No, she thought, mentally cringeing. But he knew that she wanted him. Last night her wild response to his kisses had shocked her into planning a retreat, but that had been cowardly. Rafiq was the first man she'd ever wanted—sexy as hell, considerate, intelligent, compelling and trustworthy.

Who better to be her first lover?

And Lexie made a decision—a reckless, possibly even dangerous decision—one she knew might well cause her heartbreak.

But she also knew that, no matter the grief, she'd never regret making it. Just once in her life she'd throw away caution and follow her desires.

It would be worth it, she thought, controlling the breath that came too rapidly. She turned her head, pretending to be contemplating the scenery, and knew that next time they kissed she'd— Well, she thought nervously, she'd let him realise that she didn't need to be cosseted. She was a free and independent woman, and she wanted him.

The crater lake was almost round, surrounded by thick jungle, and on one side a semi-circle of cliffs. In spite of the sunlight a faint mist hovered over it, and the only sound was bird song, faint and eerily distant.

'I can see why the legend grew up,' Lexie said, glancing around. 'It's a very potent place. Is the water still hot?'

'No, but that mist is nearly always there.' He looked down at her, ignoring the security car that had preceded them, and the bodyguard standing with his back turned as he swept the jungle with binoculars. 'I imagine crater lakes are not unusual in New Zealand.'

'There's a dormant volcanic field not far from where I live, and one of the extinct volcanoes has a crater lake, with eels as thick as your arm in it.' She gave a lopsided smile. 'It's an evocative place too, but that might be because by the time people have climbed its very steep sides they're exhausted!'

He laughed and took her elbow, steering her back to the car. 'We must go now. I have a meeting I can't miss tonight.'

They had nearly reached the castle when he said casually, 'I won't be in for dinner tonight, but tomorrow night I know of a charming little restaurant where we can eat, if you'd like to go. The chef is a genius.'

Hiding her disappointment, she told him, 'That would be lovely, thank you.'

Safely up in her room, she sighed, hugged herself, and went into the opulent bathroom to run a shower. She should, she thought, make it a cold one; for a few seconds she'd wondered whether there was any chance that Rafiq was courting her—to use an old-fashioned term.

Fortunately common sense soon banished that hope. But he couldn't fake the hunger he felt. That was genuine.

Excitement burned in the pit of her stomach, completely different from the way she'd felt when she'd realised Felipe was interested in her. She'd been flattered, and she'd enjoyed his company, had found him attractive, but it now seemed very pallid and ordinary compared to the way Rafiq affected her.

As she dried herself down she wondered what Felipe was doing. Since the accident she'd thought very little about him—when she was with Rafiq she didn't have room in her mind for anyone else.

And she was still angry with Felipe for thinking he could railroad her into sleeping with him.

Still, perhaps she should try to contact him, to tell him finally that it was over. But then he'd made no attempt to get in touch with her, and since he'd only planned to stay a couple of days, he might even have left Moraze. She'd probably never see him again, a thought that brought an unexpected sense of relief and freedom.

And as she ate her solitary dinner she recalled the warning Rafiq had delivered while they were at the perilous pool.

'I have yet to meet a woman I'd drown for...'

Odd how much that hurt.

Get used to it, she thought staunchly, because she wasn't going to play the coward's role again and change her mind.

Lexie spent the next morning in luxurious laziness with a couple of books Rafiq had sent up to her room via the maid, with a brief note apologising for his absence. One was a novel written by a famous author from Moraze, the other a beautifully produced guide to the island with fabulous photographs and a very entertaining history. She then tired herself by swimming lengths in the pool, and napped in the heat of the day, determined to be alert that night and prove that she was fully recovered from the very minor results of the accident.

For dinner she wore a sleek resort dress in a subdued gold that brought out the lights in her hair. She didn't look too bad at all, she decided, adjusting the neckline. The skirt fell to her ankles, and the sash belt clung to her narrow waist.

Tiny hot shivers tightened every nerve in her body. Later she and Rafiq would be alone together. Perhaps they'd kiss, and she'd know once more that aching, bitter-sweet delight in his arms.

And this time, instead of following his lead, she'd let him know—subtly, she hoped—that she was ready for the next step.

Whatever that might be…

Rafiq drove them to the restaurant in an unmarked car. By mutual consent they kept the conversation light, speaking mostly of the island and its beauty. A few miles inland they came to a large building throbbing with lights, and almost jumping with music. Lexie was glad when they passed it by.

He said, 'Since the sugar industry was rationalised years ago, some of the old mills have been transformed into places like this where the locals can get together to sing and dance and play music. They're now being discovered by tourists, but I thought that you might prefer somewhere smaller and more intimate. You agree?'

It was a good sign that he'd read her so accurately, though right this minute she'd probably have agreed if he'd told her the moon was falling into the sea. Sedately she said, 'It sounds perfect.'

The rest of the short journey was made in silence, although a vibrant awareness hummed between them as Rafiq turned the car down a narrow road that led back towards the coast again. Palms swayed languidly above, and the salty tang of the sea mingled with the flower perfumes that saturated these coastal lowlands. Lexie kept her eyes on the white line of the reef around a headland that jutted like a giant castle, gaunt against the star-dazzled sky.

She could wait; in fact, this slow build-up would make their kisses even sweeter, more fiery. Half eager, half apprehensive, she wondered if tonight…?

Rafiq's car was clearly well known; they were met by a man who indicated a secluded parking spot away from the small courtyard.

How many other women had Rafiq brought here? Lexie squelched the jealous little query. Live for the moment, she advised herself fiercely as she went with him into the vine-hung restaurant.

Afterwards, looking back, Lexie would always remember it as an evening of enchantment. They ate superb seafood and drank champagne, and he honoured her with his plans for the future of his country, although he first warned her, 'I'm likely to bore you.'

Lexie's brows rose. Nothing about him would bore her—and she suspected he knew it. Furthermore, she'd had enough of protecting herself. She didn't care any more. 'As a citizen of another small island nation—with about a million fewer people than Moraze—I'm interested in how you see its future.'

'I hope it will eventually be an independent and self-sustaining country under its own prime minister,' he said promptly. 'But there is some time to go before we reach that point. Democracy isn't well-established here; my father and grandfather were benevolent autocrats of the old school, so it's been left to me to introduce changes, and old habits die hard. It will probably take another generation before the reforms are so firmly bedded in that the citizens of Moraze will both choose and be their own rulers.'

'And you don't regret giving up power?'

He shrugged. 'No.' He scanned her face and said, 'The band's striking up. Would you like to dance?'

On Moraze, it seemed, ballroom dancing was the established mode. Fortunately Lexie had accompanied a friend to classes while they were at high school. If she'd known then that someday she'd be dancing a waltz with the ruler of an exotic island in the Indian Ocean, she'd have paid much more attention to the steps, she thought as she got up with him.

Heart thumping, she went into Rafiq's arms, felt them close around her, and gave herself up to the sensation. He moved with the lithe, powerful grace of an athlete, keeping perfect time. In his strong arms, his body only an inch or so away from hers, Lexie found the sexual magnetism that crackled between them both compelling and dangerously disturbing.

Part of her wanted to get these preliminaries over and go back to the castle to lose herself in this voluptuous recklessness. Another part treasured this subtle communication of eyes and senses, this aching, unsatisfied physical longing that promised an eventual rapturous release in each other's arms.

At first they talked, but eventually both fell silent; Rafiq's arm tightened across her back, and her breath came faster and faster between her lips as their bodies brushed and swayed and were taken hostage by the music.

Lexie forgot there were others there, that although the lights were dim and subdued they could be seen. Eyes locked onto Rafiq's darkly demanding ones, she danced in a thrall of desire.

He said, 'Let's get out of here.'

In a voice she didn't recognize, she said, 'Yes.'

CHAPTER SEVEN

BUT once in the car Lexie sat still, hands clasped tightly in her lap, until Rafiq ordered, 'Do up your seatbelt.'

'Oh,' she said, feeling stupid, and fumbled for it.

He said something harsh, leaned over her and found it, slamming the clip into the holder.

Lexie's breath locked in her throat while she waited for him to straighten up. Instead he bent his head and kissed her, and fireworks roared into the sky, wiping everything from her mind but this delicious, intolerable need. Her hands came out to grasp his shirt as her mouth softened beneath the hungry demand of his lips.

Until faintly the sound of an engine percolated into her consciousness. Lights flashed across her closed lids. She realised they were real lights, not the fire in her blood, and reluctantly opened her eyes.

Rafiq lifted his head. After an incredulous second he said in a raw, goaded voice, 'This is—not my usual style.' When she didn't answer he gave a ghost of a laugh and finished, 'Not yours, either?'

'No,' she admitted.

He set the car in motion, saying grimly, 'I think you must be sending me mad.'

'I know the feeling.'

He flashed her another fierce glance, then smiled, reached for her hand, and tucked it beneath his on the wheel, only releasing it when they reached a small town on the way home. Lexie let it rest in her lap, oddly chilled by the subtle rejection. Of course, it might merely be that he needed to concentrate more—but what if he was ashamed of wanting her?

Was that why he'd taken her to the tiny, out-of-the-way restaurant? After all, she was the daughter of one of the century's most despised dictators...

Oh, for heaven's sake, she thought, angrily resentful of the hurdles her mind kept setting up for her heart, he almost certainly doesn't know who your father is! And you're *not* responsible for Paulo Considine's actions.

Why should Rafiq be ashamed of her? She scrubbed up quite well, and the gown she was wearing made the most of her slim, athletic figure and her colouring. Jacoba would make her look very second-rate, but then Jacoba had that effect on every woman!

Rafiq had simply chosen somewhere discreet, and she was grateful to him for being so understanding.

And soon she'd be in his arms and her reservations would be banished.

The thought should have filled her with dismay, but although it was strange to realise that she'd lost her control so completely to a man she barely knew, she felt nothing but happiness, deep and sure and powerful.

Anyway, she was beginning to find out more about him. He was kind and thoughtful, as well as being incredibly sexy. He was also extremely intelligent, and he wanted the best for his country and his people.

She sat up straight and looked through the side window

at the starlit night. Pride was a hard thing to deal with, she thought with a wry smile, but at the moment it was all she had—pride and this unwanted, out-of-character desire that had blossomed so swiftly.

And would, she knew, come to nothing; the best thing she could hope for was for it to burn out in the fierceness of passion. She didn't expect Rafiq to reciprocate. He'd be embarrassed if he knew just how eager she was to discover what making love with him was like.

Better by far for him to believe she was enjoying a torrid affair with him, a holiday fling...

'What are you thinking?' he asked, stopping the car outside the huge doors of the castle.

'Just—drifting.' Her cheeks heated at the lie.

He switched off the engine and smiled ironically at her, moonlight outlining the autocratic angles and lines of his features. Her heart swelled, and she let herself be carried away by the wave of hunger that had been threatening to break over her all evening.

This, she thought with a desperate recklessness, was worth any pain that might lie in the future. *Anything.*

Inside the castle, Rafiq suggested a nightcap. 'We have our own distillery here. I know you enjoy wine, but at least once you should try Moraze's rum. It is mellow, and filled with the essence of flowers.'

After the first small sip, she agreed, 'You're right; it's delicious.' Tension bit into her, and she walked over to a window, clutching the glass as she gazed out onto the lagoon, that shimmered silver beneath the black sky. 'I'll always remember Moraze like this,' she said on a half sigh. 'It's everyone's secret ideal of a tropical island, filled with flowers and sunshine and laughter.'

And moonlight, and passion...

Rafiq's voice came from close behind her. 'It's not all charmingly romantic. We have the occasional hurricane, and there have been tidal waves. And although the islanders' smiles are warm, they also cry.'

She turned her head slightly, nostrils flaring at the subtle, evocative scent—pure alpha male—that teased them. 'That's life, isn't it?' she said lightly. 'Always the bitter with the sweet. But for tonight I think I'll let my inner romantic indulge herself.'

He bent his head and kissed the back of her neck, sending tiny, sexy shivers through her. 'It will be my pleasure to allow her full rein,' he said, and let his teeth graze her skin.

The shivers transmuted into arrows of golden anticipation, darting from nerve end to nerve end to summon responses from every cell in her body. Whatever happened, she had this, she thought, turning to meet his intent eyes. And for tonight, this was enough.

'Kiss me,' he commanded between his teeth. 'For hours I've been watching your mouth, imagining it under mine. Kiss me.'

Smiling, she took his face between her hands. Her fingertips tingled as they shaped out the forceful lines of his jaw, traced his beautiful, relentless mouth, travelled along the high, aristocratic sweep of his cheekbones. Excitement beat high in her, filling her bloodstream with stars, summoning a witchery of desire that ached through her in a slow, languorous tide, melting her bones.

Rafiq bent his head, and flames sparked between them as his lips came down on hers.

With an odd sigh of relief Lexie sank against him,

surrendering herself to the magic of this moment, this place—this man.

It satisfied some more than physical hunger when she felt his body harden against hers, his arms tighten, and the muted thunder of his heart drown out hers. To know that she could do this to him was an aphrodisiac in itself.

'You're sunlight and moonlight in my arms,' he said against her mouth, punctuating each word with a kiss. 'Golden and warm. Yet behind those blue, sunlit eyes there are secrets, depths as deep and mysterious as a star-shadowed night.'

'No secrets,' she said, but she'd lied and he knew it. She saw the change in his eyes.

And because she couldn't bear to spoil this, she qualified with a wry smile, 'No important secrets, anyway. Just the usual things no one wants to admit to.'

He held that mercilessly penetrating look for a moment more, then his dark lashes came down and he smiled, an almost humourless quirk of his lips.

'We all have secrets,' he said, and kissed her again before putting her away from him, and saying in a cool tone that set a distance between them, 'I think you need rest. You say you are completely recovered from the accident, but there are still traces of shadows beneath those lovely eyes.'

Although disappointment and frustration ached through her body, she smiled and nodded and went with him.

At her door he picked up her hand and kissed the palm, then closed her fingers over it. 'Sleep well,' he said quietly, and left her.

Hours later, she thought grimly that any darkness beneath her eyes was due to the time she spent awake each night, sleep driven away by highly coloured, erotic fantasies.

* * *

But when sleep finally came it somehow transmuted the keen frustration of the previous night into serene acceptance. The next day Rafiq took her for a picnic to a secluded bay on one of the royal estates. They ate in the soft, whispering shade of the casuarinas, and swam in milk-warm water, and even though they barely touched, Lexie had never been so happy. It was delicious to be given time, to feel no pressure from him at all, even though she knew he wanted her.

He made no secret of it. His glances, his smiles, the narrowed regard that set her heart pounding, all told her so. Their lovemaking, she thought dreamily as she got ready for the hotel party that night, would come when they were both ready. Until then she was content to float along in this passion-hazed dream.

Of course she wore the flame-coloured dress with its matching high-heeled sandals, and applied cosmetics with the skill and expertise she'd learned from her sister. When she was ready she stepped back from the enormous mirror and gave her reflection a swift, secret smile.

Be careful—be very careful—her mind warned, but she knew her heart wasn't going to listen. Her emotions seemed to be riding a roller coaster, the gentle acceptance of the day banished by a cocktail of adrenalin and anticipation pulsing like drugs through her veins.

At the bottom of the staircase she spared a compassionate glance for the photograph of his sister Hani. Why didn't he mention her?

Perhaps the grief of her untimely death was still too raw.

When she entered the salon, Rafiq was talking into a mobile phone, speaking with forceful authority in the local Creole French.

He looked up as she came in, and to Lexie's astonishment, and a forbidden, heady delight, she got her look—a green glitter of stunned, intense desire.

Only for a moment—he gathered himself together almost immediately—but her foolish, wayward heart rejoiced while he terminated the conversation and snapped the phone shut.

For the rest of her life she'd hug to her heart the memory of that split second of passionate hunger.

'That colour does amazing things to you.' His voice was controlled and level. 'Do you understand French?'

'No. I do speak Maori.' And Illyrian, but she wasn't going to admit to that—it could lead to questions she didn't want to answer.

They took the coast road to the new hotel. Lexie looked around her with interest when they drove in, making a small sound of pleasure at the flowers and festoons of coloured lights that decorated the place.

From beside her Rafiq said, 'There are always two openings for any new hotel on Moraze. The first is for the people who actually do the building, and then there is a more formal one, like the one you attended the other night, where publicity is a factor. That was rather stuffy; this will not be.'

The year she'd spent in Illyria had accustomed Lexie to royal occasions, but the moment she walked in with Rafiq she realised how right he was—this was indeed something special.

Smiles and cheers and applause greeted their arrival. Without the burden of being the only child of the dictator who'd terrorised the onlookers, it wasn't difficult to smile back, to relax in the warmth of their greetings.

Until she saw a face she recognised.

She must have flinched, because Rafiq demanded sharply, 'What is it? You are not well?'

'I'm perfectly all right.' After all, why on earth should she be afraid of Felipe Gastano?

He came towards them with a smile on his too-handsome face, and the air of someone completely sure of his welcome. 'Dearest Alexa,' he said smoothly as he bent to kiss her cheek.

Rafiq pulled her a little closer to his side and the unwanted kiss went awry.

Something glittered a second in Felipe's pale eyes, but the smile stayed fixed as he nodded to Rafiq. 'I am sorry,' he said in an apologetic tone that grated across Lexie's nerves. 'I was so pleased to see an old friend that I forgot protocol. Sir, it is a pleasure to be here on this auspicious occasion.'

Rafiq said, 'We're pleased to see you here.'

An apparently sincere greeting, yet somehow the calm words lifted the hairs on the back of Lexie's neck. She sensed a very strong emotion beneath his glacial self-control, and wondered if she was the cause of it.

Felipe didn't seem to notice. Still smiling, he transferred his gaze to Lexie, held her eyes a moment, then turned back to Rafiq. 'I thought I'd like to see whether my friend Alexa was enjoying all that Moraze has to offer its guests.'

Lexie stiffened, wondering exactly what he meant by those enigmatic words.

The noise level soared suddenly, fuelled by a group

of musicians who'd gathered around a bonfire blazing on the sand.

'I hope you enjoy the evening,' Rafiq said coolly. 'After a few short, official speeches there will be dancing on the beach.' His narrow smile gleamed. 'Our local dances are a feature of the entertainment here.'

'I'm sure I shall find them very interesting,' Felipe said, fixing Lexie with a significant look.

She met it with hard-won composure, both relieved and glad when he stepped back to let another couple be introduced.

As Rafiq had promised, the official part of the evening was short, punctuated by champagne toasts and much good cheer, and then the party really got going. Down on the beach, the band struck up again in impressive rhythm, guitars and keyboards vying with older instruments—a triangle, gourds with seeds inside, and an insistent drum.

'The hotel dancing troupe will do a demonstration first, but later everyone will join in,' Rafiq told her as the crowd moved onto the sand, the better to watch the spectacle. 'You will find it a little different from western dancing; in the *sanga*, people do not touch.'

Watching the dancers—women in brightly coloured cropped tops and full skirts that reached their ankles, and men in white pirate shirts knotted at the waist above tight breeches—Lexie decided they didn't need to.

Because the *sanga* was erotic enough to melt icebergs.

The women began it, holding out their full skirts while they approached the men with sensuous, shuffling steps. They swayed to the music, bare feet moving in an intricate rhythm, smiles bold and challenging as they danced from one partner to another, choosing and discarding until eventually they settled on one particular man.

When that had happened, the drum beats began to build to a crescendo and the dance took an even more provocative turn. Both women and men taunted and teased their partners, hip movements suggesting a much more intimate encounter, smiles becoming slow and languid as the dancers gazed into each other's eyes.

The insidious spell of the dance—the rhythm set up by the drums and the primitive imperative of the fire, the heat and the gorgeous, primal colours of the women's full, flounced skirts—set fire to something basic and untamed within Lexie. Her cheeks burned and her eyelids were heavy and slumbrous.

And then, with the drumbeats reaching a frenzied climax, only to abruptly halt, the world seemed suspended in dramatic silence. After several seconds people began to applaud, releasing the dancers from the erotic spell of their own contriving. Many relaxed, laughing, calling out jests to the crowd; others walked off together—still not touching, Lexie noticed.

Carefully avoiding Rafiq's scrutiny, she looked across the leaping flames of the bonfire and met Felipe Gastano's cynical smile.

She nodded, wishing she'd never been so silly as to go out with him, wishing—oh, wishing a lot of foolish things, she thought bracingly, trying to still the constant thrumming of her heart.

No wonder people talked of going troppo! This had to be the dangerous enchantment of the tropics.

As though sensing her restlessness, Rafiq said, 'Would you like to see around the hotel? The gardens and pool area are magnificent.'

'I'd love to,' she said, grateful for the chance to get away from too many interested eyes.

They walked there through a grove of casuarinas, the long, drooping needles whispering together in the scented breeze. Lexie recovered some of her composure as she admired the glorious gardens and a pool out of some designer's Arabian dream, only to lose it when they walked back to the beach and Rafiq said, 'A moment.'

She stopped with him, looking up enquiringly. He was smiling, but the intent expression of his eyes warned her what was coming, and her blood sang inside her.

Quietly he said, 'I neglected to tell you how very lovely you are.'

The kiss was merely an appetiser, one snatched before they rejoined the crowd, but she longed for more. The screen of trees was thick enough to hide them from anyone on the beach, but she hadn't thought Rafiq was the sort of man to indulge in almost-public displays.

Emerging from the feathery shade of the grove, she felt slightly embarrassed, as though everyone knew about that kiss.

From beside her Rafiq said, 'I'm afraid I must leave you for a few minutes.' A swift lift of his brows summoned a younger, good-looking man to stand beside her. 'You will enjoy discussing the dancing with Bertrand,' he said after introducing them.

Which she did. Bertrand was respectful and knew a lot about the dances of Moraze, revealing that different areas had different versions, some more restrained…

'And some—ah—less so,' he finished with a cheerful smile. 'But you won't be seeing any of *them* tonight.

Everyone is on their best behaviour because our ruler is with us.'

She encouraged him to talk about Rafiq. Not that he needed much encouragement, she thought with a wry, inner smile after five minutes. Clearly he thought his ruler only one step below the gods!

'You are laughing at me,' he said, and grinned before becoming quickly serious. 'But I am truly beholden to him. Without his intervention, I would have been cutting either sugar cane or flowers in the fields. He sits on the board that chooses the ones deserving of further education, and although I was a bad boy at school, he persuaded them to give me a chance. Everyone else thought I was beyond help; he did not. I would die for him.'

His words were simply stated, without false bravado.

'It's a lucky ruler who can inspire such loyalty,' Lexie said, meaning it. She too had experienced Rafiq's consideration and his honesty.

Bertrand drew himself up. 'It is a lucky subject who can follow such a leader,' he said. He glanced over her head and frowned. 'Oh, I will have to leave you only for a moment. I must find someone to keep you company.'

'No,' she said crisply. 'Off you go; I'll be perfectly all right.'

He dithered, then said, 'I won't be long.' After an apologetic smile, he bowed and left her.

Smiling to herself, Lexie watched him being swallowed up by the crowd as he angled towards a middle-aged woman who stood alone.

'He is one of Prince Rafiq's security men,' a voice said from behind her. 'And that woman is his superior.'

Lexie suddenly felt alone and unprotected, her skin tightening in response to an imaginary threat.

'Hello, Felipe,' she said lightly. 'I always thought security men were eight-feet tall with necks wider than their heads.'

'The muscle men, perhaps—the grunts. The others come in all sizes and shapes, and I think this one will receive a chastisement from Prince Rafiq for leaving you.'

'I'm in no danger,' she said evenly, turning her head to look up at him.

His smile was as charming as ever, his eyes as appreciative, his tone low and flirtatious, yet he left her completely cold.

'Of course you're not,' he agreed. 'But you know how it is with these rich, powerful aristocrats—they see perils in every occasion.' He gestured at the milling crowd, a little noisier than it had been before, its laughter ringing free. 'Even in such a friendly group as this—all devoted subjects.'

He transferred his gaze to her face, surveying her with an intensity that was new and unsettling. 'Did you know that the word in the bazaars is that Prince Rafiq is very interested in his house guest?'

'Rumour is—as always—hugely exaggerated,' she said evenly, and made up her mind. This wasn't the perfect occasion, but he needed to know. 'Felipe, I need to tell you—'

'Not now,' he interrupted curtly.

He wanted something; she could feel it—a fierce lust, though not for her personally, she realised with a sudden flash of insight.

It had never been her—he'd always seen her as means to some unspoken end.

Before she could finish he went on, 'And not here. It can wait until later, when de Courteveille releases you.'

'I'm not a prisoner,' she said automatically, eager to get this odd, worrying exchange over and done with. 'And I think this is as good a time and a place as any to say goodbye.'

Felipe Gastano smiled, but although the skin around his eyes crinkled they showed no emotion. 'So that is it?' He shrugged. 'Well, it was fun while it lasted, was it not?'

Relieved yet still wary, she said, 'I certainly enjoyed it.'

'I thank you. Perhaps I did not—quite—get what I thought we both wanted, but I also enjoyed our time together. However, before I go, there is something *I* must tell *you*. After your little accident, I tried to get in touch with you, but it seems you are not able to be contacted by telephone or email.'

'What do you mean?' In spite of the flames of the fire, she felt cold, and the chattering around her seemed to die away.

'Just that it seems someone is monitoring your communications with the outside world.'

'I'm sure you're wrong,' she retorted.

His smile was condescending. 'Why don't you ask de Couteveille? He comes now, and if I read him right he is not happy to see us talking together.'

Indeed, Rafiq sent her a keen glance as he approached, but although his tone when he greeted Felipe again was cool, it certainly wasn't brusque. Felipe chatted a little about the hotel development before Rafiq and Lexie moved on.

From then on they were never alone. They stayed another hour, saw another dance, this one even more sensual than the first, and then it was time to go.

On the way back to the castle Lexie was aware of a certain air of constraint in Rafiq. He was courteous, amusing, interesting—and unreachable.

Felipe's observations gnawed at her mind. She wanted to confront her host with them, yet another part of her brain told her to be sensible. Why on earth would Rafiq monitor her phone calls?

Eventually, as they drove in through the gates, she said, 'Felipe said he's been trying to contact me, but the staff were uncooperative.'

'I'm afraid they probably were,' Rafiq said coolly. 'I have people who are trained to handle the media, and they dealt with all the calls about you. I gave your sister's name to them, which is why she was put straight through, but I gained the impression that you wouldn't want Gastano to have free access to you. If I was wrong, I will of course add him to the list.'

Hastily Lexie said, 'No, it doesn't matter, thank you. He won't be calling again.' As for the emails—even if Felipe did have her correct address, they'd been known to disappear into cyberspace for days, sometimes weeks, at a time. Curiosity and a certain relief drove her to ask, 'Were there many approaches from the media?'

'Quite a few. Some of the big news agencies have stringers on the island, and of course news travels fast.' His tone hardened. 'I didn't think you'd like to be discussed in the gossip columns.'

Distastefully, she replied, 'You were right.'

Her brief encounter with gossip writers and paparazzi had sickened her of the whole industry. In Illyria she'd been shielded from the worst of their excesses, but she'd seen the havoc they could create, and she wanted no part of it. Besides, she had a feeling that if Jacoba found out she was staying with Moraze's ruler she'd send Prince Marco down to check him out.

The last thing she wanted was for Rafiq to discover who her father had been.

Honesty warred with shame. Perhaps she should tell him—right now. Yet the words froze in her throat. The sins of the fathers were indeed visited on their sons—and their daughters, she thought wearily, remembering how suspicious the Illyrians had been of her. Mud stuck; occasionally she even found herself wondering if she'd inherited any of her father's brutality.

No, much better to leave things as they were. Then Rafiq might remember her as an ordinary woman, not as the child of a monster.

Once inside the castle, Rafiq asked, 'How did you enjoy the evening?'

'Very much,' she told him, her tone more brittle than bright. 'It was interesting to meet the people who'd actually worked on the project. And their singing was fantastic.'

'What did you think of the dancing?'

His voice was amused, and his eyes half-hidden by his lashes. They were walking towards the terrace with the pavilion and the pool, and she could feel that forbidden, intoxicating anticipation chipping away at her control.

'It was very sexy,' she said firmly. 'And amazingly athletic! At times I thought they might dislocate their hips.'

He threw his black head backwards and laughed, the sound full and unforced. 'Did it give you the desire to try it?'

'I know my limitations,' she said. Curiosity drove her to ask, 'Can you do it?'

'Every Moraze-reared person can dance their version of our national dance,' he said gravely. 'Our nurses teach us it in our cradles—or so they say.'

They walked across to the pavilion, its translucent draperies floating languidly in the sea-scented breeze. A moon smiled down, silvering everything in a soft, unearthly light—the pool, the white-and-pink water lilies, the shimmering expanse of gauze that surrounded them and shut out the world.

Lexie swallowed something that obstructed her throat and said chattily, 'I think you'd probably need to learn it in the cradle to be able to do it without falling over or making a total idiot of yourself. And constant practice must be necessary to give your hips and legs that flexibility.'

'Don't be so wary—I am not like the dancers at the hotels who sometimes lure tourists onto the sand to show them how very lacking in flexibility their hips are. And to dance properly you need drums and music.' He looked down at her, his eyes gleaming and intent. 'But I would like to teach you,' he said deeply.

'Teach me what?'

'Everything,' he said starkly, and reached for her.

CHAPTER EIGHT

LEXIE swallowed again, her throat closing. He was talking about dancing, not making love. He didn't even know she was a virgin, and she had no intention of telling him.

In a voice she barely recognized, she said, 'Unfortunately, I don't think I'll be here long enough to learn—to dance, that is.'

'You're very graceful, so I'm sure you have a natural aptitude,' he said, his smile cool and subtly mocking.

'I don't know about that.' This banter with its tantalising undercurrents was new to her. Nervously she glanced away, eyes widening as she saw that the table had been set with trays of small delicacies and what was clearly a bottle of champagne.

'I thought we should toast your stay on Moraze,' Rafiq told her. 'I noticed that you didn't drink anything stronger than fruit punch at the party, but I'm hoping to tempt you with some champagne.'

Lexie knew she should refuse. In this magical glimmer of moonlit enchantment, any sensible woman would make sure her brain was in full control.

But then a sensible woman would have seen danger in

the prospect of an evening with Rafiq, and would have pretended a fragility she didn't feel. And once at the party, no sensible woman would have allowed herself to be carried away by the erotic rhythms and hypnotic drumbeats of the dancing, the whirl of colour and the open sensuousness.

And even a halfway-sensible woman would have avoided any sort of post-party drinks, and said a briskly cheerful goodnight at the door of her room before shutting said door firmly on him.

All right, so she wasn't sensible. She certainly wasn't going to walk back to the arid, lonely refuge of her bedroom.

To the crackle and heat of bridges burning behind her, she said, 'I'm easily tempted,' adding hastily when she realised what she'd implied, 'To champagne.'

Colour burned across her cheekbones and she fought back embarrassment, holding her head high and her smile steady.

One black brow lifted to shattering effect. Without saying anything, Rafiq turned to ease the top off the bottle. Instead of a pop it emitted a soft sigh—of satisfaction?

Don't even think about satisfaction! Small sips, Lexie promised herself as he poured the sparkling wine into long, elegant flutes. She'd take tiny little sips, at long, long intervals…

And when she got back to real life she'd remember this evening—this whole stay on Moraze—without regret. Instead she'd feel gratitude that the man who summoned those reckless, dangerous impulses from her was a man of honour and integrity.

'So,' Rafiq said calmly, handing her a glass, 'We drink to your continued good health.'

After one tiny, wholesome sip, she said, 'Oh, that's superb wine.'

'It is French, of course. Moraze produces some excellent table wines, but for champagne we rely on France.' He set his glass down. 'I'm glad you like it.'

Lexie made the first comment that came into her head. 'New Zealand makes good wines too.'

'Indeed it does. I have drunk a very supple, subtle Pinot Noir from the south of the South Island, and some extremely good reds from an island off the coast of Auckland.'

'Waiheke. It has its own special microclimate.'

Her innocuous words were followed by silence, far too heavy with unspoken thoughts, unbidden desire.

Desperately Lexie broke it. 'I'm no connoisseur, but I do like the wines made in Marlborough from Sauvignon Blanc grapes. In the north of the North Island, where I live, wine growers are also trying out unusual varieties of grapes to see which cope best with the humidity and the warmth.'

Oh, *brilliant*, she thought in despair. Talk about banal!

'Shall we stop fencing?' Rafiq suggested, his amused tone laced with another emotion, one that sent shivers of excited recognition through her.

'I wasn't aware we were,' she lied, hoping she sounded crisp and fully in control.

He held out his hand for her glass, and when after a moment's hesitation she handed it over, he set it beside his own on the low table. The moonlight glimmered on his white shirt, lovingly enhancing the breadth of his shoulders, the narrow waist and hips, the arrogant angles and planes of his features. Whenever she'd ridden a roller coaster she'd felt like this: both exhilarated and terrified.

'Of course we were,' he said, straightening up to smile

at her. 'We are like swordsmen, you and I, continually duelling for advantage. But it is time to bring an end to it.'

Once again her stomach did that flip thing. A hot rush of sensation drove away memories and common sense. When he looked at her like that she was aware of nothing but the drumming of her heart in her ears, and the relentless heat of desire building like a storm through her. Honey-sweet, potent as the strongest rum, powerful and frightening, it shook her to the core.

Eyes dilating endlessly, she watched his smile harden, and her breath locked in her throat at the slow slide of his hands up her arms.

'Your skin is finer by far than the silk you're wearing. For this whole interminable evening I have been wanting to touch it,' he said in a low, harsh voice, and bent his head to kiss the place his fingers had caressed.

Sharp as joy, acute as pain, pleasure shot through her at the touch of his mouth. When he slid his hands across her back and pulled her against him, she sighed his name and met his seeking, demanding kiss with open passion.

It ended too soon. He lifted his head and looked at her, green eyes glittering, and in a tone that was almost angry said, 'That is the first time you've allowed yourself to say that.'

Somehow the simple act of pronouncing the two syllables that made up his name was almost more intimate than the kisses they'd exchanged. 'You've never told me I could,' she said huskily.

A smile curved his sculpted mouth. 'I didn't know New Zealanders held to such strict rules of etiquette. In fact, I believed the publicity—that you are a laid back, ultra-casual lot.'

But her mother had not been a New Zealander, she'd

been Illyrian, and she'd brought up her daughters to be more formal than their friends.

Rafiq went on, 'We've kissed—that gives you the right to call me whatever you want.' And he kissed her again, this time lightly. 'And me the right to call you sweet Lexie—no?'

Sweet? Was he indicating that he knew she was a virgin, and that it was all right? Forcing a smile, she said, 'I don't think I'm sweet. Practical, perhaps...'

But a practical woman wouldn't be like this, locked in his arms, her body rejoicing at the hardness of his, her heart pounding so heavily he must feel it.

'Do you feel practical right now?' His voice was low and tender.

She closed her eyes against him, afraid that he'd see just what she was feeling—total surrender, a desperate, wanton abandonment of all the rules she'd lived by until she'd met him.

'No,' she admitted, gaining confidence from the thudding of his heart against her. Whatever he thought, he couldn't hide the fact that he wanted her.

'So—how do you feel?' And when she didn't answer, he laughed softly. 'A little wild?'

He punctuated each word with teasing kisses, but she sensed the inner demands driving him, and something un-regenerate and fierce flared up to meet and match his hunger.

'Reckless?' he murmured, his mouth poised so close to hers that their breaths mingled.

'Yes,' she said simply, knowing what she'd just agreed to, knowing that after this there would be no going back—knowing, and not caring, because there was nothing in the world she wanted as much as learning about Rafiq in the most intimate way of all.

Later? Oh, she'd deal with *later* when it came.

She gave a squeak of astonishment as the world swooped, and he lifted her high in his arms and carried her across to that sinful double day bed.

Beside it he lowered her to her feet, sliding her down his lean, powerful length so that his need for her became blatantly, erotically obvious. Shivering, afire with sensation, she couldn't drag her eyes away from his narrowed gaze, which darkened with an elemental need that banished all her shyness with its heat.

'This pretty dress is a seduction in itself,' he said deeply. 'I've been wanting to slide these tiny, taunting buttons free, push them back so that the silk frames you...'

As he spoke his hands followed his words. Prey to an intensity of feeling she'd never experienced, she ignored the colour burning her skin and shrugged free of the bodice. And then stopped, acutely conscious that the only thing between her breasts and his deft, insistent hands was her bra.

Should she undo it?

Almost before the thought had formulated she felt his hands at the catch—knowledgeable and far too skilful at this, she thought on a spurt of sharp jealousy that kept her head high when he eased her bra away.

He stood looking at her, the dark, fierce hunger in his eyes satisfying something primitive and untamed in her.

On a raw note, he said, 'You are—perfect,' and took her eager mouth, bending her back over his arm so that his lips slid easily from hers to the demanding, importunate tips of her breasts.

The hot caress of his mouth splintered every inhibition. Moaning, lost in a carnal haze, Lexie's hands clenched helplessly in the fine fabric of his shirt as his mouth worked erotic magic on her.

'No,' she muttered when he lifted his head.

'What?'

He bit it out with such harshness she forced her eyes open, and saw the sudden rigidity in his features. 'Don't stop,' she said on a gasp.

But he held her eyes in a measuring stare. 'You are sure?'

'Of course I'm sure.' Frustrated, she stumbled over her next words. 'If you stop, I just might kill you.'

Strong arms closed around her again, and he set her on the bed. Shivering with anticipation so keen it came close to pain, she watched him shuck off his shirt. Lamplight gilded his skin, picking out the smooth swell and flex of muscles as he dropped the garment to the ground. But when his hands moved to the belt of his trousers she looked away, suddenly and shyly aware of her total lack of experience.

Should she tell him? Would he think she was some sort of frigid freak? Worse still, would he be overcome by an outdated chivalry and refuse to make love to her?

Clamping her mouth to hold back the confession that threatened to tumble out, she kicked off her shoes, not caring whether they landed on the stone terrace beside the bed or in the pool a few feet away.

Lithely, Rafiq came down beside her, muscles shifting and coiling, a study in gleaming bronze power. Lexie swallowed to ease a dry throat as the sheer size of him struck home. Without the civilising influence of his superbly tailored clothes, the difference between her female slenderness and his forceful masculinity overwhelmed her.

But that initial qualm was immediately eased by his gentleness as he began to slide the dress down her body.

Only to stop when he saw the faint shadows on her ribcage. She said quickly, 'They've just about gone now.'

'I don't want to hurt you.' He bent his sleek black head and kissed them, his lips sending darts of sensation to her very soul.

'You couldn't hurt me.' When he hesitated, she held her breath in an agony of supplication.

He said, 'I will be very careful, and you must tell me if there is any pain.'

'I will.'

Her eyes flew open in dismay as another thought presented itself. What if he thought she was using contraceptive medication?

As though he'd read her mind, he asked, 'Are you protected, my sweet one?'

'No,' she mumbled, rigid with embarrassment.

'It is no problem.' He got off the bed.

Lexie knew she should be relieved, and was shocked to discover that the thought of carrying Rafiq's child sent a subversive pang of longing through her.

Keeping her eyes away from what he was doing, she looked downwards. Her gaze stopped on the thong her sister had insisted she wear under the silk dress.

Should she take it off?

Colour mantled her skin, and desire ebbed under the weight of her embarrassment. How on earth did people ever make love with all these things to think about?

'What is worrying you?'

It was scary just how easily he could read her. 'Nothing.'

But once she was in his arms again, and his mouth on hers wreaked the familiar havoc to her busy mind, the need came back, swift and sure and compelling. Her virgin fears and worries vanished in an intense, voluptuous craving for something only Rafiq could give her.

'You taste like desire,' he said. 'Warm and silken and mind-blowing.'

His hand touched her breast, and she was unable to prevent a convulsive jerk of response.

'What is it?' he demanded.

'I just… I can't… I want you so much,' she finished in a rush, scarlet with an odd sort of defiance, but determined to be honest.

His laughter was deep and intimate. Her hips thrust upwards in an involuntary plea and demand for something she craved so much she could feel the wanting in her bones.

Against her skin, he murmured, 'So fierce you are, so responsive, so passionate, my dove. But shy—I won't break if you touch me.'

Almost dazed by the ferocity of her need, she smoothed a hand over his chest, her fingertips tingling at the resilience of his skin, the subtle shift and move of the muscles and tendons, their power and promise.

'Yes,' he whispered, his warm breath tantalising the sensitive tip of her breast. 'Touch me, Lexie, as you want to—and as you want to be touched.'

Cautiously she ran a coaxing, tentative hand across his shoulder, her fingertips thrilling at the heat of his fine-grained skin, the coiled strength that called to something deep inside her. Her breath came quickly; she bent her head so that her hair fell across him in a golden-amber flood, and then she kissed the path her fingers had made, rejoicing at the sudden thunder of his heart.

Emboldened, she opened her mouth and licked him, savouring his taste—a hint of salt, faint musk, all vital male.

Passion was a painful flame, an exciting demand, a surge of sensation through her so intense it was all she had room for. She said in an aching voice, 'You are beautiful.'

'Ah, no.' Rafiq sounded oddly shaken. 'That is for me to say to you. But *beautiful* does not convey enough—you are lithe and graceful, a woman of flame and satin and desire. The moment my eyes found you, I knew that this was inevitable.'

And he kissed her again, banishing her final fears and worries so completely that she willingly followed wherever he led, her body arching in uncontrollable urgency as he showed her what pleasure points lay in her breasts, her waist, the tiny hollow of her navel, the sleek curves of her hips…

And the removal of the thong became an erotic experience that almost banished all of her shyness.

But when his black head moved lower, she stiffened. He dropped a final kiss on the plane of her stomach and looked up, his eyes unexpectedly keen.

Colour flooded her skin. Rafiq smiled slowly, almost cruelly, and stroked one lean, long-fingered hand from the hollow of her throat. A thread of fire followed that deliberate claiming, radiating between the high peaks of her breasts, across her stomach, finally erupting when he cupped the wildly sensitive mound at the junction of her legs.

It was a gesture of pure possession—a statement of ownership—and oddly it gave Lexie a confidence she'd never have achieved otherwise.

Eyes holding his, she mimicked the sweep of his hand,

letting her fingers linger on the antique pattern of hair across his chest, discovering the small, masculine nipples. The dark flush across his high, patrician cheekbones made her even bolder; she slid her palm across his flat, taut abdomen, relishing the hardening of muscles beneath her touch.

Narrow hips beckoned. Carefully, lovingly, she outlined them, bending to kiss the lean contours of his body.

And then her confidence faltered, faded. He was acutely aroused, and she literally didn't know what to do next.

He laughed quietly, darkly glittering eyes registering her embarrassment without censure. Silently he moved his hand and, as she bucked beneath his probing fingers, he found the passage that waited for him so eagerly, and explored it with a gentleness she found unbearably stimulating.

A soft, almost guttural sound broke past her lips. Gripping his shoulders, she felt the slickness of sweat beneath her hands, but this time she was too lost in the shatteringly sweet sensations he was conjuring to understand what was happening to him.

She needed—her whole body yearned for—*something*. Connection, completion, she thought inadequately, a unity she could only imagine, yet it was what she'd been waiting on for these long years past.

'Rafiq,' she breathed, her fingers clenching on him as he moved over her.

'Yes, my sweet one. Wait just a little time.' His voice was laboured, hoarse, as he turned away.

Lost in the turmoil of her senses, she closed her eyes, but when he poised himself over her again she opened them, and slid her hands down his back to his hips, then smiled and pulled him down.

He dragged in a harsh breath. His half-closed eyes locked with hers, so that she thought she was falling into the centre of a green firestorm, as he slowly, carefully, eased himself into her.

For a split second pain threatened, and she tensed, but then he broke through that tiny invisible barrier. Shivering, she felt sensation flood through her in a wave of heat, of joy, of seeking that something wonderful that still lay ahead of her, and again she arched into him in speechless supplication.

Rafiq's jaw clenched and, as though her movement had snapped the last shred of his self-control, he pressed home with a single, powerful thrust. Almost sobbing with pleasure, she soared at each welcome intrusion, up and up, and over a barrier into an ecstasy that shook the foundations of her world.

Almost immediately he followed her into that rarefied region, and when his climax was over he asked in a raw voice, 'Why the tears, my lovely girl?'

'I didn't know,' Lexie said unevenly, surprised to find that she was crying.

He rolled over onto his side, raising himself on one arm to look down into her face. Shaken to her centre, she closed her eyes, because she couldn't see anything in his expression to match the tumult of emotions rioting through her— a kind of relief, fierce exultation, wariness, and a sweet exhaustion.

Obviously he felt nothing like that; once more he was fully in control, the arrogant framework of his face even more pronounced, the green eyes hard and accusing.

'Was that the first time you've had an orgasm?' he asked.

Flushing, she turned her face away, and resisted when an inexorable finger turned it back. He didn't hurt her, but she knew he was scanning her face for every nuance, every fleeting emotion.

'Look at me,' he commanded.

'No.'

Her heart thudded in the silence, until he said, still in that cool, controlled tone, 'Or was that the first time you've made love?'

He couldn't know. There was no way he could know. There had been only one swiftly vanishing second of pain...

But why did it matter so much to her that he shouldn't know?

'Is it important?' she parried, wishing her voice wasn't so thin.

No muscle moved in his face, but her heart quailed. However, his tone was grave when he replied, 'I think it is, if it was the first time for you. I could have been gentler—?'

'I didn't want *gentle*,' she flashed, determined to put an end to this hugely embarrassing conversation. Weren't men supposed to roll over and go to sleep after sex?

But then, Rafiq de Courteveille wasn't like other men. In that moment she realised that she was in even greater danger than she'd imagined.

The danger of falling in love, if she hadn't already done so.

In words brittle with desperation, she said, 'I'm sorry if it wasn't—'

'Hush.' He stopped the tumbling words with his mouth, in a kiss that brought every emotion and thought to a crashing halt, vanquished by the turbulence of sensation and remembered rapture.

Rafiq lifted his dark head so that his words were spoken against her lips in the lightest of kisses. 'It was—' He paused, as though choosing what to say next, then went on, 'Much more than I expected. I hope that for you it was good too.'

CHAPTER NINE

LEXIE breathed, 'It was wonderful. Couldn't you tell?'

Rafiq's smile was wry. 'Some women fake orgasms very well, but yes, I could tell. I'm glad.'

And without saying anything more he got up and stooped for his clothes, giving her a last view of his powerful back and leg muscles shifting in smooth harmony, the light of the lamps casting golden highlights and coppery shadows over his lean, magnificent body.

He looked both alien and heartbreakingly familiar, a man of sophistication backed by raw power, his combination of bloodlines and cultures so different that the only thing they had in common was this passionate desire.

Lexie's heart clamped into a hard knot in her chest. What now?

Without hurrying, he got into his trousers and slung the shirt over one broad shoulder. She couldn't read his expression; he'd retreated behind the bronze mask of his face to a place where he seemed entirely unaware of her.

Chilled, she sat up and reached for her dress. Perhaps the movement broke his introspection; he came across and picked it up from the floor to put it beside her.

'Not a good way to treat such a pretty thing,' he said conversationally, his eyes hooded and enigmatic, and walked away to the table where the champagne flutes gleamed in the lamplight.

Hastily scrambling into her clothes, Lexie wondered dismally what on earth she was supposed to do now.

What followed was a tense ten minutes spent in sophisticated conversation with Rafiq—conversation Lexie could match only with taut, disconnected answers.

So she felt relief and disappointment in equal measure when he walked her back to the door of her bedroom.

There he paused, and said with a humourless twist of his lips, 'This is not how I envisaged the end of the evening, but I think we both need a night of sleep before we talk.'

Eyes raking her face, he finished, 'Before that, I should repeat that I enjoyed very much our evening together—all of it. I hope you did too.'

She flushed, wanting only to be taken in his arms again, to be reassured in the most basic of ways that he was telling her the truth.

But that wasn't going to happen. 'I've already told you I did,' she said, her tone aloof and edged with more than a hint of defiance.

He laughed softly, and for a transparent second she thought he was going to put paid to the tumbling whirlwind of her thoughts and emotions with another sensuous kiss and the addictive security of his arms.

Then his face closed against her, and he stepped backwards with an inclination of his head. 'Goodnight. Sleep well,' he said formally.

'Goodnight.' She closed the door on him before the hot tears could reach her eyes.

As always he'd been considerate, but even though he'd liked making love to her he might still be regretting that it had happened. After all, there was a huge difference between an experienced woman of the world, who knew how to conduct an affair with style and grace, and a virgin with no skills or experience when it came to matters of sex.

He might even now be trying to find a way to tell her that it was over—a kind, *considerate* way, of course—she thought on a spurt of fresh anguish.

She woke the next morning with one decision fixed in her mind: she'd go back to the hotel.

'No,' Rafiq said unemotionally when she told him at breakfast on the terrace that overlooked the lowlands.

Lexie's brows shot up. Pleased with the cool crispness of her tone, she stated, 'I'm not asking your permission. I'm perfectly well, so the hotel no longer has any reason to object.'

He leaned back. A stray ray of sun struck across his face, and she glimpsed a corsair, dark and dangerous—a leader of men even more desperate then he was.

'It is not possible,' he said evenly. 'Your accommodation has been given to another guest.'

Stunned, she closed her mouth with a snap. 'Who made that decision?'

'I told them to,' he said with a controlled assurance that grated across her nerves. 'The hotel opening was a huge success—bookings have come in from all over the world. It would have been foolish not to take advantage of that. Why do you want to leave the castle?'

'Because there's no longer a reason for me to be here.' She stared at him, her eyes sending a challenge she didn't care to voice. 'My stay was only ever temporary. I'm fine, my ribs are fine—' Colour burned her skin but she ploughed on, 'As you know.'

When Rafiq got to his feet in one swift movement, she had to stop herself from flinching. He loomed, and although Lexie knew she had nothing to fear from him she had to resist her immediate impulse to leap up so that she faced him on slightly more equal terms.

He was deliberately being intimidating, she realised, her hand closing around the handle of a knife. *Why?*

Calmly, yet with an edge of authority to his voice as though reasoning with a rebellious teenager, he said, 'There is no need for you to go. I understand your feelings, and I agree—this has happened so fast that we don't know each other very well. But fleeing is not the way to deal with it.' His eyes dropped to her death grip on the handle of the butter knife. 'I refuse to believe that you are afraid of me.'

'I'm not!' She dropped the knife back onto her plate. The sharp little chink broke into the soft air like a small explosion.

No, she wasn't afraid of him; she just wanted him so much that her last shreds of prudence dictated flight, before she made a total fool of herself by falling madly and hopelessly in love with him.

'Perhaps you should be,' he said, and the silence between them became suddenly charged with a menace that sent shock waves through her.

Disbelievingly, she stared at him as he leaned down and caught her wrist, urging her upwards. His mouth came down on hers; she resisted for a second, then sank into his warmth and strength, even as part of her mind fought this insidious entrapment.

The sensations—potent, arousing—were the same, yet

she knew something was different. Behind his passion she sensed an icily restrained anger and a determination that made her extremely wary.

When he released her she commanded furiously, 'Don't ever do that again.'

He examined her with hooded eyes, flinty and cold. As she watched the anger faded, and he said something in a raw, harsh voice in the local language.

Lexie didn't have to understand it to know that he was swearing.

Between his teeth he said in English, 'I will not touch you again until you ask me to.'

'I— All right,' she snapped, hoping her uncertainty wasn't humiliatingly obvious.

He scanned her face, his own devoid of expression. 'I am not normally so crass,' he said curtly. 'You affect me in a way I haven't had to deal with before. I'm sorry.'

Lexie bit her lip, trying to repress a forlorn hope. Surely he couldn't mean that he was as lost to emotion as she was? She didn't dare hope that.

His eyes hardened. 'Tell me, do you want to leave because we made love?'

After a few tense seconds she decided that the truth was the only way to go. 'Yes.'

Not because of their loving—never *that*—but because afterwards the odd sense of alienation, of rejection, had pained and confused her.

Rafiq watched her expression, still shuttered against him, and wished again he'd managed to rein in his hungry desire. Making love had infinitely complicated the situation; he felt smirched by his own behaviour, although it had never occurred to him that she could be a virgin.

He couldn't let her leave the castle because Gastano still wanted her, and he was dangerous.

After witnessing that carefully stage-managed kiss at the party last night, the self-titled count must know he'd lost his passport to the world of the very rich and privileged. During the past twelve hours he'd have learned that his world was shattering around him, the empire he'd built with such ruthlessness in chaos, and Interpol hot on his heels.

And although he might not yet know that the man who'd taken Lexie from him was responsible for all that, he would very soon. He'd react with all the viciousness of a cornered rat.

Warning her would achieve nothing; she clearly had no knowledge of Gastano's criminal life, and why should she believe Rafiq?

Unless he told her about Hani…?

Not now, he thought. Everything in him refused to reveal his sister's humiliation and suicide. But although he hadn't been able to protect her, he could make sure Lexie was safe.

Choosing his words carefully, he said, 'I promised a few moments ago not to touch you until you asked me to. I made that promise in anger, but it holds. You will be perfectly safe here.'

Lexie sensed rather than saw the inflexible line of his mouth, and wondered what was going on behind the handsome, arrogant features.

Fighting back a bleak disappointment, she said, 'I know that. It's— You were right, everything's happened so quickly…'

So quickly it didn't seem possible that the emotions that gripped her could be true. Until she remembered that her sister had taken one look at Prince Marco of Illyria and instantly fallen into lust.

And although that initial fierce attraction had grown into love, just because it had happened for Jacoba didn't mean it was going to be her fate too.

Rafiq smiled, and the green eyes—so uncompromising a minute ago—warmed. 'It will be difficult keeping my hands off you, but by the exercise of great—*immense*—restraint I think I can manage it.'

And he lifted her hand to his mouth and kissed it, then turned it over to press another kiss into the palm.

A painful delight throbbed through her. Somehow their lovemaking the previous night had made her even more sensitive, as though she'd been trained to react infinitely more strongly to his powerful presence.

If she were cautious or even sensible, she'd leave the castle and find a room in another hotel. She'd run fast and far—as far as New Zealand—from this reckless delight.

But she wasn't going to. Whatever happened she would always be glad that she'd met Rafiq, that her initiation to sex had been so wonderful, that here on this magical island east of Zanzibar she'd found something rare and precious, something she wasn't going to let fear forbid her.

'Perhaps,' she said solemnly, those swift kisses still tingling through her bloodstream. 'But how do you know I'll have the same self-control?'

'I rather hope you don't.' The deep voice was amused and tender. 'But not today; I have a council meeting that will take all day. So relax.'

He didn't come home until after she'd gone to bed, but he'd rung twice, and at the sound of his voice she'd melted.

Rafiq. Always and for ever Rafiq, she thought later, lying in bed alone and watching the stars drift slowly across the velvet sky as she remembered the previous night. Eventually she slid into sleep, and into turbulent dreams.

Several hours later Rafiq asked abruptly, 'Where is M'selle Sinclair?'

'She went up to her room shortly after she had dinner, sir.'

'Thank you.' He strode up the staircase, slowing a little when the passage forked to go to Lexie's room.

Damn, he wanted her! After that moment's hesitation, he went on past. In his own room he swore beneath his breath when he saw the red light blinking on the communication device that connected him to the head of security.

'Yes?' he barked into it.

'Sorry, sir, but there's just been an attempted robbery in the strongroom at the citadel. It looks like an inside job on the fire-diamond vaults.'

Rafiq's head came up. Harshly he ordered, 'Go on.'

He listened keenly as she concisely laid out the evening's events. 'A man armed with the correct passwords infiltrated the citadel and got as far as the vaults before the alarms finally picked up his presence.'

Mind racing, Rafiq demanded, 'Where is he?'

Chagrined, she admitted, 'He gave us the slip in the old town.'

So he was a local. No outsider would be able to navigate the narrow alleys of the original town.

Mme Fanchette confirmed this. 'We've got a good shot of him on tape. He's a petty thief—been in trouble since he was a kid, and he's now deep in hock over gambling debts.' She paused. 'The man he owes has been seen talking to Gastano.'

Rafiq digested that. 'Have the passwords been changed?'

'As we speak.'

'But if we don't know who the traitor in the household is, we'll have to assume that he—or she—will also be told of the changes.' His frown deepening, Rafiq thought rapidly before commanding, 'I want the watch on Gastano reinforced; he's wily and he's ruthless. And step up the security at the castle as well as the citadel.'

'You think M'selle Sinclair is in danger?'

'Possibly.'

Driven by a need to know that Lexie was safe, Rafiq strode down the hall towards her room. Once he was sure of that, he'd set a guard at her door. Although he'd chosen her room to make sure she couldn't escape, the sheer walls on the seaward side would also make it impossible for anyone to reach her that way.

But if Felipe Gastano had suborned someone in the household to get those passwords, he could have access to someone in the castle as well.

Rafiq opened the door quietly. The room was in darkness, although the shutters were still open. He could see the stars through the tall windows, and hear the muted thunder of the sea on the reef.

And something else—a soft weeping that lifted the hairs on the back of his neck.

Get out of here, he told himself, angry because he knew he wasn't going to abandon her to such distress.

His voice woke Lexie from a nightmare of loss and dis-illusion, of frantic fear and terror. She reached blindly for him, feeling the side of the bed sink as he sat down on it, and then the safe haven of his arms closed around her.

Stroking her hair, he murmured, 'Hush, hush, it's all right, Lexie. It's just a nightmare, just a bad dream, and you're awake now.'

'You were gone,' she sobbed. 'I couldn't find you—they wouldn't let me go—but I knew you were dead…'

'I am very much alive.' His confident voice eased the horror that still gripped her. He picked up her hand and held it against his heart. 'Feel that? It's my pulse, and it's not going to stop for many years yet.'

Brokenly, mouth against his throat, she said, 'Oh, thank God. Thank God…'

And she reached up and kissed him, relief making her bold.

When he pulled away, she whispered, 'No. Oh, please.' And his mouth hardened on hers and she knew it was going to be all right.

They made love with a rapacity that should have shocked her, and then slowly, gently, with a sweet tenderness that made her heart sing and weep at the same time.

When he eased away from her, she clung openly.

Rafiq laughed, a sexy sound that sent more shivers of delight through her. 'So valiant now,' he teased, and ran a light, infinitely provocative finger from the hollow at the base of her throat to the dimple of her navel.

Lashes drooping over her eyes, she savoured the rills of anticipation from that light, unsatisfying touch. She looked up into a face that hardened subtly, the autocratic framework exposed by tanned skin.

I love you so much, she thought achingly.

She kissed along his jaw, lips tingling at the slight

friction of his beard while heat began to build again in the pit of her stomach.

'Yes,' he said deeply. 'You like that. So do I.'

His seeking hand cupped the soft mound of her femininity, then two fingers slid into the moist recess and she arched against the intimate caress, her breath coming rapidly between her lips, the heat transmuted into a wildly erotic complex of sensations.

But this wasn't what she wanted—a quick release.

No, she wanted him to remember her, to never be able to walk into this room again without her face coming to him, and her voice echoing in his ears.

Emboldened, she pushed at his shoulders. 'Lie down,' she said, and bent her head and kissed him, using that slight leverage to ease him back.

She felt his mouth curve beneath hers, and then he obeyed, settling onto the sheets, heavy-lidded eyes smouldering.

Long and lean and golden, he sprawled across the bed beneath her, the smooth definition of relaxed muscles beneath his sleek skin belying the power she knew he commanded, the blazing male potency that called to everything female in her.

Absorbed in sensation, she explored him with increasing boldness, delighting in the contrast of textures and the swift contraction of muscles beneath her fingertips, the way his eyes promised the most carnal of retribution, the thinning of his beautiful mouth as he fought her effect on him.

A film of moisture across his forehead sent her pulses racing. She lowered her head and touched tiny butterfly kisses there, then licked across the path her lips had taken.

Hoarsely, he said, 'You're killing me.' And when she hesitated his mouth twisted and he went on, 'But stopping would kill me faster.'

'I just want to please you.' She dropped another kiss on each shoulder, bunched now, and iron-hard beneath her seeking mouth.

He gestured down his body. 'You must see you're succeeding.'

Indeed she could. Desire burned her cheeks, and she reached out a hand, cupping him, caressing the silken shaft that had given her such erotic pleasure.

He said unevenly, 'Much more of that, and you'll unman me.' His arms were outstretched, the muscles corded and tight, his hands curled into fists.

'I don't think anyone could unman you,' she said in a tone to match his, and opened her lips to his fierce demand, before a wild impulse pulled her away to climb over him and stretch herself the length of his taut body.

He didn't move, not even when she slid herself down, shivering with pleasure as she took him into her. She caught the green glitter beneath his lashes, welcoming the colour along his high, autocratic cheekbones.

Concentrating hard, she began to clench and unclench inner muscles in a subtle massage. His lashes lifted; he pinioned her gaze with such single-minded intensity, she felt he was reading her soul.

Eyes locked, bodies still, the only sound was the mingled harshness of their breathing. Lexie continued the voluptuous torment, ratcheting up the sensual tension, until the only thing she could feel was the molten pleasure rising like the tide through every cell.

And then it broke over her, a wave of such passionate

delight that she gave a muffled cry, and her body stiffened in a rictus of ecstatic release.

Rafiq's hands whipped up to support her; he made a guttural sound that mingled with hers, and his powerful length arced beneath hers, hands on her hips forcing her down as he joined her in fulfilment.

When it was over he held her against him and they lay spent in silent communication. Dazed, Lexie understood that something significant had happened, but she didn't know exactly what. It seemed to her that they had forged a link that might never be broken.

For her, anyway.

Much later, when she was almost asleep, she felt him move. Grief tore at her; without thinking, she whispered, 'Stay with me.'

But he said gently, 'My sweet one, I don't want the staff to know I have been with you. Let me go now.'

Humiliation woke her properly. Keeping her eyes closed, she mumbled, 'Oh, of course.'

Rafiq heard the note of chagrin in her voice and gritted his teeth as he dressed. All he wanted was go back to her, lose himself in her warmth and her passion, but he needed to check the castle security.

Something he should have done *before* he came to her room.

When Lexie woke the next morning it was to a lonely breakfast out on the terrace. Forcing fresh fruit salad and toast past her lips took effort and concentration.

She'd asked where Rafiq was, and had been told that he was working at the citadel. Well, of course; rulers had to rule, and no doubt that was what Rafiq did every day.

But once more she faced the bitterness of rejection. Was she being too sensitive? Probably. Last night had been the high point of her life so far, yet clearly to him it had meant so little he hadn't even bothered to join her for breakfast.

'Stop it,' she muttered, startling a small bird that had settled on the edge of the balustrade. Her mouth quirked as it opened its bright orange wings and fluttered to a safer perch on a potted gardenia not too far away. 'Sorry, birdie, it's not your fault.'

This was all so new to her, but obviously it wasn't to Rafiq. And she'd been the lucky recipient of his overdeveloped sense of responsibility, so she shouldn't be surprised or disappointed at his absence.

She was finishing a cup of delicious local coffee when she heard the chatter of a helicopter coming fast from the capital.

A pang of embarrassment clutched her. What had seemed so natural and thrilling last night suddenly appeared in a different light. Would Rafiq think she'd been forward and needy when she'd writhed in desperate rapture in his arms? Or when she'd explored his body with greedy adoration? Or, most pathetic of all, when she'd pleaded with him to stay with her?

Was he secretly despising her? Or wondering how to get rid of her?

And did he realise—as she had when she'd woken that morning—that their mutual passion had been so great they'd forgotten to take any precautions against pregnancy? She'd counted the days of her cycle, relaxing when she found it was highly unlikely she'd been fertile, even though the thought of carrying Rafiq's child under her heart melted her bones.

Heat stung her skin. She got up and walked nervously to the shade of an arbour, watching the black dot that was the chopper grow rapidly as it headed purposefully towards the castle.

Should she go down, or wait for Rafiq here?

She decided to wait.

The maid Cari appeared, obviously looking for her. And just as obviously flustered, holding her handbag. 'Miss, it is the Emir—he has sent the helicopter to pick you up. From the upper terrace!'

Joy flooded through her. 'Oh—I'd better go, then!'

Wondering why on earth Rafiq had chosen that particular landing ground, she accepted the bag and hurried with the maid up onto the upper terrace, where the water lilies held their satiny cups up to the sun.

Noise filled the air and she had to half close her eyes against the wind blasting from the rotors as the chopper landed. Someone inside pushed back the door, painted with the stallion of the royal house of Moraze in all its menace and grace, the crown on its head glittering with fire.

The same man beckoned. Without hesitation, Lexie ran across.

Strong hands hauled her inside and stuffed her into a seat. The chopper took off instantly, and the door closed before she had time to fix her seatbelt. Frowning, she did up the belt and turned towards the man next to her.

An odd apprehension kicked her beneath the ribs when Felipe Gastano lifted a thumb to her and mouthed words she couldn't hear.

CHAPTER TEN

GASTANO'S smile broadened as Lexie shook her head and put her hands to her ears. When he tossed her a pair of earphones she clapped them on, only to realise they weren't connected to the communications system.

Ice touched her skin. Something, she thought feverishly, was wrong. Rafiq didn't like the count; he wouldn't have sent him for her.

Her eyes flicked to the man piloting the chopper. He wore an official flying suit, the emblem of the rearing horse clear on it. Only this horse had wings. Chastened, Lexie let out a small huff of air.

She was being over-dramatic. After all, what on earth could there be to be afraid of? This was a Moraze Air Force helicopter, and the pilot was clearly a serviceman. Besides, Felipe was no threat to her.

So why did she now feel an instinctive unease in his presence?

Folding her hands tensely in her lap, she looked down at the countryside, the green of sugar cane fields giving way to the jungle of the escarpment. Perhaps Felipe had been offered a chance to see the famed horse herds?

Indeed, once they'd reached the plateau, she leaned forward and to her delight saw a herd below. They didn't seem alarmed; after a quick gaze upwards they resumed grazing, as though the helicopter was a regular sight in their sky. For some reason, that made her feel better.

But when the chopper headed for a collection of buildings, she frowned as it banked and dropped towards the ground.

It looked like ruins. Some sort of industrial complex, not very big—a sugar mill on a back country road, perhaps. Indeed, when she looked down she could see that there had once been a house there, but it had been burned to the ground.

Startled, she searched for signs of people, but nothing moved in the shrubby vegetation around the stone buildings. The cold patch beneath her ribs increased in size.

What was going on?

The chopper landed with a slight bump and a whirl of dust. The engines changed pitch, and Gastano indicated that she get out.

Lexie made up her mind. She shook her head.

Felipe's smile widened. He groped in a bag at his feet to produce a small, snub-nosed black pistol that he aimed straight at her.

The colour drained from her skin. Instead of words the only sound she could make was a feeble croak of disbelief, and then something hit her, and in a violent pang of pain she lost consciousness.

Lexie huddled on the stone floor, reluctantly accepting that this was no nightmare; tied at the wrists and the ankles, she was propped up against a wall in what looked like an abandoned sugar mill somewhere in Moraze. Forcing herself to ignore the thumping of her head and the nausea, she tried to work out what had happened.

Why had Felipe snatched her from the castle?

A swift glance revealed that she seemed to be alone, but instinct stopped her first impulsive attempt to free her hands. Instead she strained to hear—something, *anything!*

But the only sounds were placid, country noises—a distant bird call, low and consoling, and a soft sigh of wind seeping through the empty windows, sweet with the fragrance of flowers and fresh grass.

A second later she stiffened. A faint whisper—alien, barely there—grated across nerves already stretched taut. Lexie froze, trying to draw strength from the solidity of the stone building, the fact that fire and desolation and the inexorable depredations of the tropics, hadn't been able to turn it into a complete ruin.

That faint, untraceable sound came again and once more she strained to pinpoint it. Was it a thickening of the atmosphere, a primitive warning that bypassed more advanced senses to home in on the inner core that dealt with raw, basic self-preservation?

Or was she fooling herself?

Slowly, carefully, hardly daring to breathe, she inched her head around. Nothing moved in the gloom, but she knew she wasn't alone in the shadowy building. There were plenty of places to hide—behind the wreckage of machinery seemed the most likely.

Footsteps from outside swivelled her head around. Rafiq, she thought in anguish, wondering how she knew it was him. If her senses spoke truly, he was walking into a trap. Surely he wasn't alone? Panic knotted her stomach as she tried to work out what to do.

Scream a warning? But was that what Felipe wanted? He hadn't gagged her.

The footsteps stopped, and her mind ricocheted from one supposition to another. Possibly Felipe thought he'd hit her hard enough to keep her unconscious for longer.

And knowing Rafiq, he'd come in whatever she did, she thought, stifling her panic. But surely—oh, God, *surely*—he wouldn't come here alone and without weapons?

Head pounding, she struggled to hear more.

And caught it—the barest whisper of motion from outside the doorless building.

Lexie bit down on her lip. Rafiq had to know she was here; he wouldn't have come otherwise. She mustn't call out.

But oh, it was so hard…

A jerky flow of movement caught the corner of her eye. Not breathing, she whipped her head around and saw the dark figure of Gastano take a step from behind the machinery so that he could see the doorway more clearly.

Her heart juddered to a stop when she realised he was still holding the pistol. So he meant to kill Rafiq.

Everything else forgotten, she opened her mouth, only to have her yell forestalled by Gastano's voice, bold and arrogantly satisfied.

'So you came, de Courteveille. I knew you would—stupidly chivalrous to the end.'

For a second Rafiq's silhouette in the open door shuddered against the light, then blended into the dimness inside.

Lexie closed her eyes, nausea gripping her. That moment of clarity had revealed he carried no weapon.

And then he spoke, his voice cool and dispassionate. 'Now that M'selle Sinclair has fulfilled her function as bait, I suggest you let her go. She's not necessary to you any longer.'

With a wide smile, Gastano strolled over to stand above Lexie like a conqueror. 'I have no intention of letting either of you go until you agree to my terms. Come closer—you are too far away.'

He's getting off on this, Lexie realised with sick fear.

And he was totally confident that he held all the cards.

Holding her breath, she watched Rafiq move silently towards them. It was too dark for her to see his face, but she could tell from his gait that he was ready for anything that might happen. She opened her mouth to tell him that Gastano was armed, but was forestalled by her captor.

Sharply he said, 'That's close enough.'

Rafiq took another step, and Gastano swung the pistol around until it was directed straight at Lexie. He swung it back to fix onto Rafiq, and said between his teeth, 'You will do everything I say, when I say it, or suffer the consequences. Take one step backwards.'

Rafiq didn't move, and Gastano prodded her with his foot. 'If you do not, then Alexa will die,' he said calmly. 'Oh, not now, and not quickly—she will die at my disposal. The same way your sister did.'

Hani? Into Lexie's mind flashed the photograph of the girl, vivid, bright, her face full of impudence and joy. Rafiq's sister. And Gastano? Bile caught in her throat.

Gastano's eyes never left his antagonist's face, and she could feel the confidence oozing from him. 'It was quite clever of you to realise that I had plans for Alexa. But you underestimated me.'

Gastano's laugh was a taunt as he switched his gaze back to Lexie for a second.

'You should perhaps have been a little more careful of her feelings before you made love to her, *sir*.' He pronounced the last word with a gloating emphasis that made it an insult. 'Women are inclined to be upset when they are made use of so flagrantly. But I'm sure she suspected that there had to be an ulterior motive to your lovemaking. Alexa knows she is no beauty—unlike your charming but so naïve sister.'

And while an appalled and horrified Lexie was digesting this, he finished on a sneer, 'Besides, you are no better than I am. You decided that the best form of revenge would be to seduce the woman I intend to marry. You were wrong—I still intend to marry her, and neither you nor she will prevent it.'

The fear gripping Lexie slowly receded before an icy realisation. She thought she heard her heart break, shatter into a thousand brittle pieces in her breast, each one stabbing her with a pain that would never go away.

At the centre of this war between the two men was Gastano's treatment of Rafiq's sister.

Lexie herself was merely a bystander, a pawn used by both men in a battle that had nothing to do with her. Rafiq's lovemaking must have been a coolly calculated move to at least shake what he thought might be her loyalty to Gastano.

But he'd come to rescue her.

Rafiq stood like stone, his hands clenched at his sides, his eyes never leaving the man. 'You bastard,' he said gutturally, his voice low and shaking with fury, hands so tightly clenched Lexie could see the whiteness of his knuckles in the gloom. 'You'll rot in hell for what you did to Hani.'

Gastano shrugged dispassionately. 'She had choices,'

he said with callous indifference. 'No one forced her into my bed. No one forced her to take drugs or to prostitute herself so that she could pay for them.'

Ruthlessly Lexie pushed the choking sense of betrayal to the back of her mind. Rafiq had to have some sort of plan. And here on Moraze he had the advantage of local knowledge.

The count understood that too, so he was pushing Rafiq, trying to get him off balance. But a glance at Rafiq's face, drawn and darkly anguished, shook her.

It appeared Gastano was succeeding.

Yet although Gastano might pretend to despise Rafiq he was watching him closely, his finger poised on the trigger of the revolver.

As long as he kept that unwavering focus, Rafiq was in danger.

Her pulses quickened. 'I wouldn't marry you if you were the last man in the world. You're just a gutless big-noter,' she said contemptuously.

Gastano swung around. At any other time she might have laughed at the shock in his face, but as soon as the pistol wavered from its lock on Rafiq, she lashed out with her bound feet, catching the count more by luck than good judgment on the side of the kneecap.

He lurched sideways, his finger tightening on the trigger. Ducking reflexively, she felt the wind of the bullet against her cheek. Her eyes clamped tight shut and her heart pumped so loudly she couldn't hear anything else.

A choked sound forced her eyes open in time to see Rafiq fell Gastano with one blow. The count went down into a limp heap; Rafiq dropped on one knee to check him out, then got up and headed towards her in a lethal, silent rush. She gasped as he grabbed her and hurled her brutally behind what seemed some sort of press.

'Are you all right?' he demanded, running his hands over her with a gentleness so at variance with the brutality of the blow he'd delivered, she could only stare dumbly at him.

A flurry of shots echoed through the building.

'Silence,' Rafiq growled into her ear, shielding her with his body as she struggled to get up.

A voice called out in the local language. Rafiq answered, holding her still as a man raced around the side of the vat.

His answer to Rafiq's swift question was one succinct word.

Rafiq eased up, supporting her while he rapped out an order. The newcomer pulled a knife from somewhere on his person and handed it over, and Rafiq slashed the cords that held her wrists and ankles together.

Chafing her wrists gently, he said, 'You are safe now.'

'I'm all right,' she muttered, still stunned by the abrupt change of situation. She dragged in a sharp breath as the blood began to return to her hands and feet.

'He fooled me into thinking he was truly unconscious.' Ignoring her shivers, he began on her ankles, his fingers soothing yet firm. 'I should have been more careful. He had a knife, and was heading for us when one of my men shot him. It was too quick a death for one so foul, but the best outcome, nevertheless. Otherwise he'd have had to be put on trial.'

Intuitively Lexie guessed why he hadn't wanted that— the details of his sister's degradation would have become common knowledge. He needed to protect her reputation.

She opened her mouth to speak, and he demanded, 'Did he hurt you in any way?'

'Except for hitting me on the head, no,' she said huskily.

He swore harshly, then demanded, 'Were you unconscious?'

'Yes.'

'Do you have a headache now?' He leaned forward and raised her eyelid, staring intently and impersonally into her pupils. 'No, they don't seem dilated, but you could have concussion. Stay still.'

Frowning, she said, 'I did have a headache, but I feel better now.'

'Adrenalin,' he said, getting to his feet.

Desperate to know, she asked, 'Tell me, who—how did whoever shot him get here?'

'There are three army snipers here. The plan was that I should keep him occupied while they crept into place, but you put paid to that. They had only just got here when you lashed out at him—we were lucky one got a clear enough sighting to be able to knock him down.'

'I see,' she said numbly, wincing as feeling cascaded painfully back into her feet and hands. 'How did you get here so quickly?'

His expression hardened. 'He sent a message from the helicopter. I came up in another one.'

A man came through and said something. Rafiq shook his head and gave a swift order, then got to his feet.

'We will soon have you out of here,' he promised, and moved noiselessly away.

Feeling sick, she eased back against the wall, dragging the damp, slightly musty air into her lungs. It smelt sweet and thick and heavy with the scent of past sugar harvests, the faint, spirituous flavour making her gag.

She realised she was shivering; icy tremors seemed to

soak right down into her bones. Shock, she thought distantly, and set herself to mastering it. By the time Rafiq came back she'd managed to regain enough composure to control everything but her chattering teeth.

'Don't try to talk,' he commanded as he picked her up and carried her out towards the waiting helicopter.

Back at the hospital she had a shower, a medical checkup that revealed she didn't have concussion, and an injection to counter any infection in the abrasions around her wrists and ankles.

Also, she strongly suspected the next morning, waking up in the hospital bed, some sedative to give her the night of dreamless sleep she'd just enjoyed.

Late that morning she was sent back to the castle in a limousine, with a very solemn Cari and a bodyguard.

She didn't see Rafiq for another two days. He sent her a note saying that because of the fallout from Gastano's death he'd be busy, and that he wanted her to do nothing but recover.

Misery ate into her, but she told herself stoically that she needed time to get her strength back—strength to leave Moraze and Rafiq without making an idiot of herself.

On the morning she woke with a clear head, she said to Cari, when the maid brought her breakfast tray, 'I'm getting up today.'

'Yes, the doctor is coming this morning to make sure you are recovered.' Carefully Cari positioned the tray over Lexie's knees.

Lexie opened her mouth, then closed it. She knew it was no use fighting Rafiq's dictates. And anyway, it was sensible to get an all-clear. 'And after that I'm getting up properly.'

Instead of leaving, the maid stood, her hands held tightly behind her back. In a subdued voice she said, 'If I had thought just a little I would have known the helicopter was not sent by the Emir. He would never have told it to land on the terrace.' She bit her lip, anxiously scanning Lexie's face. 'I thought it was so romantic. I am truly sorry.'

'It's all right,' Lexie said hastily. 'You weren't to know. Don't worry, Cari. Apart from this bump on the head, I wasn't hurt, and all's well now.'

But once alone, she pushed the tray away. Although she felt the effects of Gastano's wickedness like a smeary feather brushed over her spirit, it was Rafiq's betrayal that shattered her.

She took a deep breath because she just had to accept that, grit her teeth and get on with life. If she faced facts and kept her head high, she'd cope.

But although she'd always known that he didn't love her, it hurt in some shrinking, vulnerable part to know that his actions had been a cynical exercise in revenge. Poor fool that she was, she'd treasure the memories for the rest of her life, but Rafiq? Well, after she'd left Moraze, he'd probably never think of her again.

Or only as the unwitting agent of change who'd helped him avenge his sister's death.

Stoically she forced down breakfast and endured the medical check-up, which resulted in a complete clearance. It took all of her strength to smile and thank the doctor. When she got back to New Zealand she could indulge in whatever form of breakdown she preferred, she thought drearily, but until then she had to stay in control.

Late in the afternoon, Rafiq came to see her. After

she'd satisfied his queries about her health, she said firmly, 'I'm ready to go home now. Can you recommend a good travel agent?'

He paused, then said, 'There are some things I need to explain to you.'

Rapidly, before he had time to go further, she said, 'Look, it doesn't matter. I understand why you did what you did. Your sister—'

Not a muscle moved in the arrogant face, and his voice was cool and flat as he cut her off. 'My sister died because of Gastano. I suspect he targeted her for the same reason he chose you—because she had access to a world he desired above everything else. Also, he enjoyed defiling innocence.'

Humiliated, she stared at him. He was almost certainly right.

Stone-faced, Rafiq said, 'Did you know he was a drug dealer?'

'*No!*' Her skin crawled.

He searched her face keenly. 'Did he ever offer you drugs?'

'Once,' she said quietly, so appalled she felt physically ill. The conversation in the ruins had played through her mind over and over, and she'd accepted that Felipe must have had something to do with the drug trade, but the thought still horrified her. 'I didn't think he was a user, but I supposed that he knew how to get them. Even in New Zealand drugs are easy enough to get if you really want them. It never occurred to me he was a dealer.'

Rafiq's brows drew together. 'Sit down,' he commanded, and when she stayed defiantly upright he caught her up and carried her to a chair.

In the strong grip of his arms the familiar magic washed

over Lexie, drowning out everything but aching need and memories of passion. Until Rafiq deposited her onto the chair, with care but no tenderness, as though he couldn't wait to get rid of her.

Hope died a wretched death. She could have crossed her arms over her breasts and rocked with wailing despair, but pride kept her upright, steadied her gaze, forced her lips to move. 'Do you believe me?'

'Of course,' he said with a faint air of surprise. 'Like all men of his stamp, Gastano could read people—it must have been obvious to him that you were not a good candidate for addiction.'

'Was *he* an addict?'

'No. As you heard in the old sugar mill—' He paused a moment before finishing in a level, emotionless tone, 'He turned my sister into one.'

'I'm so sorry.' Totally inadequate though her words were, it was all Lexie could think of to say.

Still in that clinical, dispassionate tone, he went on, 'When she realised that the man she thought she loved had deliberately betrayed her and seduced her, she could not live with the pain and humiliation and she committed suicide.'

Lexie said again, 'I'm so very sorry.'

'She was eighteen at the time, in her first year at university.'

CHAPTER ELEVEN

THE nausea that had slowly dissipated over the past couple of days returned to Lexie in a rush.

Rafiq continued in a flat, lethal tone, 'Gastano didn't know that before she died she sent me a letter telling me about their secret affair, her dependence on the drugs he'd fed her, and her shame and humiliation and horror at her foolishness. He believed I knew nothing about him, which gave me the edge when it came to hunting him down.'

His air, his voice, even his measured words, gave no hint of his attachment to his sister—but she could see a little below that controlled surface now, and she understood his bleak determination to bring Gastano to book.

Not only did she understand it, she thought bleakly, she applauded it.

If only it hadn't cost her her heart.

Rafiq's voice was cool and clinical. 'Gastano is— was—the kingpin of a cartel that shipped heroin and cocaine to Europe and North America. He was assessing Moraze as his next staging post.'

Rafiq had spent the past days and most of the nights working with his government and the security service. He looked at Lexie's intelligent face and thought wearily that, just for once, he wished she'd accept the easy answer.

But that wasn't Lexie. And he owed her the truth before they moved on from this.

'He was an arrogant man, vain and secretly insecure,' he said austerely. 'Possibly because he was illegitimate; the title he used was not his but his half-brother's, who died in suspicious circumstances.'

Horrified, she demanded, 'You mean—did he *murder* his brother?'

'I don't know. I think not—but the real count died of a drug overdose.'

'Nothing—not growing up illegitimate, not *anything*— excuses dealing in drugs.'

She stopped, acutely conscious that her own father had killed without compunction, and spent years plundering a country at the whim of inner demons that nothing else could satisfy.

Rafiq filled in her sudden silence. 'Who knows the secret workings of a man's mind?' he said sombrely. 'I'm not sorry he is dead, not sorry I've spent the past two years working to bring him down. His damned drugs have killed more people and ruined more lives than anyone can count.'

He paused, and she looked up to meet his narrowed eyes. 'But I am very sorry you were caught up in it. That was never my intention.'

'I understand now why you acted the way you did.' she said abruptly, 'I didn't know he planned to marry me. I had no intention of marrying him.'

Soon she'd leave Moraze, and once she got home she'd be able to put this behind her, she thought. How could she blame Rafiq for doing what he could to protect his subjects and his sister's memory? He wouldn't be the man she loved if he'd done anything else.

His seduction of her might have been coldly calculated, but set against the misery and degradation that Felipe had already caused, and the prospect of him using Moraze as a staging post for his filthy merchandise, she couldn't blame Rafiq for using whatever weapons he had.

She looked at him and asked slowly, 'Did you know he planned to marry me?'

'I learned of it after you came here,' Rafiq said curtly.

'If you knew that, you must have known I wasn't in any danger from him. Why on earth did you come unarmed to the sugar mill?' Lexie asked, furious with him all over again for taking such a risk.

'It wasn't as dangerous as it seemed. I was almost certain he wouldn't kill me.'

'How could you be so sure?' she demanded, her voice angry. 'You had no right to put yourself at risk like that!'

He sent her a sardonic glance. 'To my knowledge he had never actually murdered anyone himself. There was always someone to do it for him, you see. It is much easier to say "get rid of this person" than actually do the act yourself. Besides, after seeing me kiss you the night before, he judged that he could use you as leverage to force me to do what he wanted here on Moraze. I couldn't allow that to happen.'

He frowned, and she felt her heart bump into overdrive, singing with a painful joy because she loved him. He didn't love her; it was his overdeveloped sense of responsibility that had brought him to her rescue.

In a hard voice he resumed. 'The snipers had a fix on him—you didn't need to recklessly throw yourself in the path of danger by kicking at him.'

'*You* were the reckless one,' she retorted, stung. 'You had no weapons, and just acting on the hunch that he wouldn't kill either of us was sheer madness.'

His broad shoulders lifted. 'It was a desperate situation,' he said calmly. 'Besides, Moraze has been my responsibility for more years than I care to count; I owe it much.'

And there, she thought wearily, was her answer in a nutshell: everything he'd done, including seducing her, had been for the honour of his sister and the protection of his country. *Everything*—their passionate lovemaking, the hours of honey and fire in his arms, the slow discovery of each other—had been an unspoken lie.

For him. Not for her. She was leaving her heart in his keeping—unnoticed, unwanted, but lost to her for ever.

Rafiq's face hardened even further. In a cold, controlled voice, he said, 'I will not insult you with excuses for my actions. At first I suspected that you were his lover—'

'With no proof,' she flashed.

His eyes didn't soften. 'It seemed more likely than not. And I deliberately manipulated circumstances to separate you from him—partly because, although I knew him to be dangerous, I didn't know how he'd react when he realised that his empire was shattering around him.'

'And partly to keep his mind off the fact that it was happening,' she said, engulfed by intense tiredness.

His mouth compressed, but he agreed calmly, 'That too.'

'It was a clever move, and it worked. He must have been furious when he realised you were just as capable as he was of separating sex from the things that really matter.'

She'd intended her words to cut, but Rafiq shrugged them off without any visible reaction. 'I must also apologise to you.'

Pride wasn't much armour, but it was all she had left, and it drove her to forestall the inevitable. 'I'm glad you achieved what you wanted. And although it's a terrible thing to say, I can't be sorry that Felipe is dead.'

Because she suspected that Rafiq would never have been safe if the other man had lived; the count's ego and malice would have seen him work to bring down the man who'd bested him.

She hesitated. 'It gives me the creeps to know I once thought he was fun to be with.'

'He traded on his charm and his *savoir faire*.' He dismissed Gastano with a single movement of his hand and looked at her. 'Forget about him. My government and I have worked hard to contain the fallout from all this, and succeeded in great part. Now that it is over, there is one thing left for me to do.'

Eyes widening, she watched him come towards her, his eyes hooded and unreadable in his hard face. Her heart began to beat faster, and the hope she'd thought so dead burst into flames inside her. Uncertainly she said, 'What— what is that?'

He stood for a moment, looking down at her with a hooded gaze. Was he going to suggest they continue their affair?

What would she answer? Part of Lexie wanted nothing more than to lose herself again in the fiery passion summoned by his lightest touch. But any affair with him would eventually end, leaving her bereft.

He said gravely, 'I have never done this before, so perhaps I am clumsy, but I would like very much for you to marry me, Lexie.'

Sheer untrammelled joy fountained through her, and then—as quickly as it had come—faded. The photograph of his sister, virginal and betrayed, flashed in front of her eyes.

He'd been shocked and startled to discover that Lexie had never had a lover. And Gastano's jibe that seducing Lexie made him no better than the count would have stung.

Scanning his composed face, she searched for some sign of love, something akin to the violence of her own emotions. Her heart quailed when she read nothing. He even looked slightly amused, as though he knew what she felt, and expected nothing more than her vehement agreement.

What she couldn't see was any sign of tenderness, of love.

It was then that Lexie realised that there are worse things than a love betrayed. A treacherous little hope whispered that in time Rafiq could learn to love her—only to be quickly rejected. Lexie's hungry heart wanted more than a comfortable, sensible affection.

Oh, it would be a reasonably suitable marriage, she thought bitterly; after all, even though her father had been a murderous monster, she was related to one of the oldest ruling families in Europe.

She had no money and few social graces, but hell, her sister had learned how to cope with life as a princess; she could too.

Only she wasn't going to.

A *sensible* marriage? Never! She longed for the fiery incandescence of uncontrollable love, the sort that lasted a lifetime, a love that would match hers.

In a subdued voice she told him, 'It's a great honour, but I'm afraid I can't accept.'

Rafiq's expression didn't change. If anything, more was needed to convince her that he felt nothing more for her than a convenient passion, it was this.

He said on a note of irony, 'Perhaps I need to convince you.'

And he pulled her into his arms, locking her there with relentless desire. Fighting back a white-hot hunger, Lexie drew on all her strength. She had to stop this before it went any further—and she knew how to do it. Rafiq's icy pride was a weapon for him, but also a weak point.

Quietly, her voice level and bleak, she said, 'You can make me want you. But when it's over, I'll still refuse your proposal.'

Then, because her emotions threatened to burst through the dam of her own pride, she folded her lips, trying fiercely to project her utter conviction.

To her astonishment he smiled and bent his head. She expected a kiss that echoed the violence of her emotions, but when it came, it was a soft whisper of sensation across her lips that broke through her defences, so raggedly and hastily erected.

Against her mouth he said softly, 'Are you going to refuse me, my dear one? Surely you can't be so cruel…?'

'Please,' she whispered, aching with anguish. 'Don't do this to me.'

'But see what you do to me.' His voice was tender, yet she heard the satisfaction in it as he pulled her a little closer so that she could feel the wild response of his body, lean and hard and supplicant against hers.

This, she thought, was truly the end. She looked at him, her eyes glittering, and said between her teeth, 'All right, then—one last time, and on my terms. I'll be leaving Moraze tomorrow.'

He froze, his eyes narrowing as he looked down at her. 'You mean this?'

'Yes. It's over, Rafiq.' She lifted her head high.

He knew he could manipulate her with sex—and she couldn't bear the thought of a loveless marriage, based only on that. When he became accustomed to her, as he would, would there be other women?

Perhaps not; he was an honourable man, but she would not be seduced into an existence that would eventually result in a kind of death of the spirit.

'It might not be,' he said curtly. 'There is the fact that last time we made love we did not use any protection. That was my responsibility, and I failed you.'

With steely determination, she said, 'It's highly unlikely that I'm pregnant, but the possibility is no reason for marriage.'

'What better reason for marriage can there be?' he demanded, his face like stone.

Lexie had to respect him for not lying to her, but oh, if he'd said—just once—that he loved her she might surrender.

He'd carefully avoided that.

Hoarsely she said, 'If I am pregnant, I promise I'll let you know.'

'If you are pregnant you will marry me,' he returned with icy authority. 'My child will not grow up illegitimate like Gastano.'

'Our child—if there is one—will not grow up like him at all! What do I have to do to convince you that I know what's best for me? And it's not marriage with you. I will *not* be harassed or coaxed or seduced or intimidated into it.'

Just in time she stopped herself from adding, *Your sister might have died because she was betrayed, but I'm not quite so weak.*

It would be spiteful and it would be wrong, because her will power was already fading.

He said, 'I could stop you from leaving Moraze.'

'You wouldn't dare!' She stared at him, and something cold slithered the length of her spine. He looked ruthless, as tough as any of his ancestors of old, capable of anything. 'Yes, you would,' she said slowly, heavily.

She bared her teeth at him. 'If the sex—because that's all you'd get—is so important to you, then I can't see why we shouldn't enjoy each other one last time before I go.'

Silkily he answered, 'No reason at all. But once you leave I'll hold you to that promise. If you are pregnant, I want to know immediately.'

Colour flooded her skin, then vanished. Dismissing the immediate outcry from some distant, barely heard part of her that must be common sense, she said crisply, 'Of course.'

And she lowered her lashes to mask the anguish in her eyes, and kissed his throat.

His familiar taste summoned an instant response, hot and compelling and heady, a surge of desire that swept through her and obliterated any weak appeal to prudence and caution, and all the boring concerns that might stop her making love to Rafiq before she walked out of his life.

'I'm glad we understand each other so well.'

Something cynical and dangerous in his tone lifted the hairs on the back of her neck, but before she had time to react he lifted her and carried her across to the huge bed.

Mouth on hers, arms tight around her, he lowered her so that her feet came to rest on the carpet.

'So,' he said coolly, holding her a little away from him, his eyes intense and compelling, 'Indulge me. Strip for me.'

His smile stirred more bitter pride in her. 'Only if you do it for me as well,' she retorted, head high, eyes challenging him in the most elemental of battles.

'Perhaps we should do it for each other,' he suggested. He kissed the spot where her neck met her shoulder, and then bit delicately, his teeth sending frissons of excitement through her.

So they did, interspersing the removal of each garment with kisses that grew more and more urgent, with caresses that banished her inhibitions—until in the end they came together in a conflagration of reckless hunger so intense Lexie burned up in it, her body an instrument of such extreme pleasure she forgot everything but the violence of her own sensations as he made himself master of her every reaction.

Her ecstatic release scared her; she lay panting in his arms, shocked at the strength of her feelings, her body still hungry for something he couldn't give her.

When she could speak again she unclenched her hands from the sheets and whispered hoarsely, 'You didn't—you haven't...'

Her voice trailed away as she met his eyes. Ruthless, utterly determined, they made her flinch. 'Not yet,' he said, his voice harsh and raw. 'Not yet, my dove, my beautiful woman...'

And he began all over again. That searing, primal look warned her. She braced herself to be plundered, but this time—ah, this time—it was slow and erotically voluptuous. Like the conqueror he was, he made himself master of her body, his hands coaxing, his mouth taking its fill of the satin perfection of her breasts, of every inch of her skin except for the place that longed for him.

Frustrated, she reached for him, but he pushed her hands above her head and held them in a loose grip while he bent his head to continue the exquisite, gentle torture, knowing with experience and a sure male instinct which were her most sensitive pleasure points, exactly how long to work each one, and when to leave and find the next...

Helpless, she began to whimper with anguished pleasure, muttering, 'Please—oh, please, Rafiq—now... now...'

And then he took her in a stark, slow thrust; almost she convulsed around him, but he eased out, leaving her bereft, aching with loss, until he took her again, this time even deeper, even slower...

She struggled, but he said steadily, 'It is hard, I know, but wait. Just wait.'

So she did, and he continued his slow, erotically charged strokes until at last she could hold back no longer. Her body arched uncontrollably—she cried out his name as ecstasy swept over her and through her.

After he'd left her she wept for his cruel tenderness, his total, complete consideration and absorption in his exploration of her body, the way he'd skilfully coaxed her into ecstasy before sending her soaring beyond it into a place she'd never been before.

And would never find again, she knew. For the rest of her life she'd long for that place, the security of his arms, the knowledge of his hunger for her—and know that it wasn't enough.

She wanted his love: total, unconditional, without strings. The way she loved him.

And as she couldn't have it, she'd just have to learn to live without it.

* * *

They met the next morning for an oddly formal farewell.

Lexie thanked him for his hospitality. In turn, he thanked her for her help, and finished, 'I ask you not to speak of what has happened here.'

'Of course I won't,' she said rapidly. When she got home she was going to try her hardest to forget everything about the island. She met his keen, intimidating scrutiny with a direct look. 'And you don't have to thank me—I did nothing but complicate things!'

'You kept your head in a situation that must have terrified you.'

With an irony that hid the sound of her heart cracking again, she said, 'I should have known—actually, I did know—that you had a plan. I was just afraid that he might kill you before you were able to carry it out.'

For a second she caught a glimpse of that desert ancestor, autocratic and powerful and ruthless. 'Thank you.' Without pausing, he went on, 'I want to hear from you as soon as you know whether or not you are pregnant.'

'Very well.'

He said with an undernote of menace, 'Don't put me to the trouble of coming after you, Lexie.'

She stiffened. 'Don't worry about that,' she said pleasantly. 'I won't.'

Their eyes locked. 'I'm glad,' he said with silky distinctness. 'If at any time or place you need help—whatever sort—contact me.'

'Thank you,' she said, knowing it meant nothing. Oh, if she asked, he'd move heaven and earth to do what he could for her, she was quite sure.

But she'd never ask.

He smiled, its irony echoing hers. 'Thank you, Lexie. Goodbye.'

And it was over. She was taken to the airport in a discreet car and settled into a first-class seat. As the huge jet lifted over the grasslands, she watched a herd of horses galloping, galloping, galloping, and thought bleakly that at least she'd seen them.

The shrill summons of her mobile phone woke her from a deep sleep. Wearily, she groped for it and muttered, 'Hello?'

'Lexie, get out here fast. Sultan's Favourite's in trouble.'

Exhaustion fled in a rush of adrenalin. 'What?'

'The foal's not coming easy.'

'Be there in ten.'

Fingers clenched on the steering wheel, she drove through the night to the stables owned by a good friend of hers. 'How is she?' she demanded on arrival, scanning the mare—who, she was grateful to see, looked as comfortable as any female could in her condition.

It was a condition Lexie didn't share. She'd been back in New Zealand for a month—long enough to establish that she wasn't pregnant. As soon as she'd known, she'd sent a formal registered letter to Rafiq to tell him that he was free of any prospect of fatherhood. His reply had been equally formal. He wished her everything good in her life. And he was sincerely hers, Rafiq de Couteveille.

The irony wasn't lost on her, but she'd suppressed the pain, forcing it down until it was merely a deep-seated ache. Sometimes it came to the surface in dreams of loss and anguish, but mostly she could function as though she'd never been anywhere east of Zanzibar.

'I think she's OK now,' her friend said with a wry smile. 'I panicked.'

But the mare needed help, and it was almost dawn when Lexie drove back home. Fortunately it was the weekend and she wasn't on call, so she could go back to bed once she got home.

Sleep didn't come easily anymore. She wondered how much longer she was going to be tormented by this fierce hunger for a man who'd used her. How was it that film stars and the glamorous people who filled the gossip magazines seemed able to flit from lover to lover without wasting time on grief?

No such luck for her. She rolled over onto her back and stared at the ceiling. She'd hoped that the aching emptiness inside her would soon dissipate, but so far time had only intensified it. Fill her days with work as much as she could, she still missed Rafiq.

One day she'd see a notice of his engagement to some suitable woman, and then she'd be forced to get on with her life.

A week previously she'd decided she'd had enough. Mourning a love that had never had a chance was a futile waste of time; from now on, she'd ignore it and live life to the full instead of moping like some Victorian heroine intent on devoting the rest of her life to the memory of a lost love.

So when a newly separated partner in her practice asked her to accompany him to a formal dinner, she'd accepted. He was a dear, and still very much in love with his wife, so she didn't fear any sort of advance.

But if she wanted to stay awake during the dinner with him the following night, she'd have to get some sleep!

Eventually she dropped off, enough so that concealer

hid the shadows under her eyes, and the evening passed pleasantly enough.

'Thanks for coming with me,' her date said on the way home. 'I'm not looking forward to Christmas. What are you doing?'

'I'm on duty,' she said cheerfully.

He nodded as they turned into her gateway. 'I enjoyed that evening more than I expected to. Thanks to you, mainly,' he said. 'Lexie, if it's an imposition say so, but do you mind if I make use of you shamelessly for this festive season? There are several other functions I can't get out of...'

She'd had more enthusiastic offers, but she understood. She too had functions she couldn't avoid. 'OK,' she said lightly, and opened her door.

But he got out and came around the car to her. 'I'll see you to the door,' he said with a wry attempt at a smile. 'I haven't entirely forgotten how to behave.'

He waited until she'd unlocked it, and then said, 'I enjoyed tonight so much I'm quite looking forward to our next date.'

Lexie waved as he turned the car and set off down the drive again. It was a beautiful night, and she stood for a few seconds to admire the stars, thinking of the same stars in a depthless tropical sky.

Stop it, she told herself fiercely, and stepped back.

Then froze as a piece of shadow detached itself from beneath the jacaranda tree and came towards her.

'Just as well he didn't try to kiss you,' Rafiq said in a lethal voice.

The initial flash of terror was superseded by a triumphant joy so fierce that she pressed one hand over her heart. As he strode silently towards her in the starlight, she couldn't speak.

And when she did her voice was thin and uncontrolled. 'It's none of your business who I kiss.'

He stopped just in front of her. 'You really believe that?' he asked in a low, fierce growl.

And at her defiant nod he said thickly, 'Then you need to learn otherwise,' and hauled her into his arms, his mouth coming down on hers with a famished hunger that smashed through every shaky defence.

Passion soared through her, unleashed and formidable, sweeping away common sense and all the rational arguments she'd used to bolster herself through the long, dark days since she'd left Moraze.

But when at last he lifted his mouth from hers, and framed her face with his lean strong hands, eyes fiercely intent as he scanned her, she asked beneath a harsh indrawn breath, 'What are you doing here?'

'I am starving to death without you,' he said just as quietly, but with an intensity that brought warmth, and a wild hope with it.

CHAPTER TWELVE

'RAFIQ,' she said on a broken little sob. 'I don't want an affair.'

He said jaggedly, 'I cannot bear your tears. Rage at me, little cat, show me the spirit you've kept intact all through this. But I beg you, don't weep.'

Lexie couldn't control her shock. His unexpected arrival had finally tipped her over the precipice she'd been negotiating for the past weeks. She gulped as more tears clogged her throat, and then she felt the longed-for strength of his arms around her, his warmth enclosing her as he rocked her back and forth, murmuring soft, comforting words in the language she didn't understand.

Until finally her tears slowed and she could think again.

Then he said deeply, 'So it has been as bad for you as it has for me?'

'I don't know how bad it's been for you,' she retorted with a flash of spirit.

He tipped her chin and examined her face, a gleam of satisfaction gilding the dark green eyes. 'Very bad,' he said succinctly. 'Until you left, I didn't realise how much I was going to miss you. I hoped you were missing me just as much, but if you were, you didn't show it.'

'How do you know?' she demanded, startled by his words.

He looked arrogantly sure of himself, a conqueror fully in command. 'Surely you didn't think I would let you go so easily?' he asked, his brows lifting. 'Of course I made sure you were all right.'

'You had me watched?' Lexie tried very hard to be outraged; it shouldn't have been difficult, but her natural anger was softened by a treacherous glow of pleasure.

'Checked,' he corrected, his jaw jutting. 'If you had been happy, if you'd showed no signs of missing me, then I would have accepted your decision.'

She tried to pull back; he held her for another second, then let her go. 'Really?' she said disbelievingly.

Shrugging those broad shoulders, he conceded with an enigmatic smile, 'Not without seeing you again. Everything happened so fast between us, and then you discovered that I had used you, and naturally you were furious and hurt. And there was the possibility of a child to complicate the situation. You needed time to think, to regroup, to discover for yourself what your emotions were. But always I planned to come and ask you to marry me again.'

Lexie heard his words as though in a dream. She stared at him and said furiously, 'Just what do you feel for me? Apart from passion?' Colour heated her cheekbones, then faded abruptly, so that they stood out starkly beneath her hot blue eyes. 'That's not the best base for something as serious as marriage, but you've never shown any indication of feeling anything more.'

He looked at her as though she was mad, his eyes blazing above a face suddenly stark. 'I love you,' he said between his teeth. 'Of course I love you—how could you not have known? I asked you to marry me, Lexie!'

'You asked me to marry you because you found out I was a virgin,' she retorted tensely, her heart thudding so hard she had to focus on speaking clearly. 'And because you thought I might be pregnant!'

Her whole future depended on this. He had to be sure—as sure as she was. And she had to be sure, too, that his sister's wretched fate hadn't driven him into that astonishing proposal.

Because it had to be faced, she said more steadily, 'You couldn't bear to be associated with Gastano in anything, especially not the seduction of a virgin. And then we made love without protection.'

Appalled, she watched his hands clench at his sides. He surveyed her with menacing eyes, their glitter so intimidating she had to stop herself from taking a step backwards. After a few seconds, he dragged in a deep breath and his fists relaxed.

'I did not *seduce* you,' he rasped. 'We made love. There is a difference. For me there was always love.'

'I can't believe that,' she said desperately, wanting so much to accept what he was saying she could feel the need like a huge hunger inside her. 'You despised me because you thought I'd been Felipe's lover.'

'I tried very hard *to* despise you,' he corrected with a grim smile. 'From the moment I saw you in that flirtatious orange dress, I wanted you, but even then I felt more for you than the transient lust of a man for a sexy woman.'

'How do you know?'

He gave her another arrogant look, one mingled with frustration, then, in a gesture as brutal as it was unexpected, hammered a fist into one cupped hand. 'I felt—doubt, confusion, anger. All those—and something else. For the first time in my life, I did not know what it was I was feeling, and the loss of control made me angry.

'So, yes, I suspected that you were far more experienced than you were, but the woman I kidnapped did not live up to my expectations. You were warm and thoughtful; after the car crash, you insisted on finding out how the driver of the car was, and you sent her a card and flowers. She is one of my best agents, by the way. You showed no signs of interest in anything but Moraze and the horses, the people—almost everything around you but me!'

Lexie couldn't stop her incredulous laugh. 'You must have known—you're an experienced man, and every time you touched me or kissed me, I lost it.'

His anger faded. He smiled, but with irony. 'Ah, but you regained that infuriating composure very quickly. I would like to be able to tell you when love happened, how it happened, but it came so swiftly, stealing my heart before I knew it was in danger. Even after we made love the first time, I thought I was safe. Until in the sugar mill, when it seemed that Gastano held all the cards in his hands, and I knew that if I couldn't rescue you I would die a lonely man.'

That simple statement and the tone it was delivered in—as stark and uncompromising as the stripped anguish in his eyes—almost satisfied Lexie's desperate need to be convinced.

Yet still she couldn't quite dare to believe him. Instead she turned and unlocked the door, saying over her shoulder, 'You'd better come inside. It's summer here, but it must be cold for you after Moraze.'

What would he think of her cottage? He followed her

in, closing the door behind him. She stood silently, devouring him with her eyes, as he inspected the small living room with its doors opening out onto a brick terrace.

'It looks like you,' he said at last, then turned and smiled at her. 'Warm and practical, yet with charm and spirit. When did you know you loved me?'

'I knew for sure when I thought Gastano was going to kill you. That's why I kicked out at him; I realised that life without you wouldn't be worth living.'

Rafiq held out his hand. She took it, and his fingers closed around hers, warm, confident, strong and protective. But he didn't take her into his arms.

Instead he said in a low, implacable voice, 'I loathed Gastano for what he did to my sister—he stripped her of her innocence, degraded her until she believed that she was worth nothing. But I didn't feel that I had done that to you after we made love. I felt—transported, as though this was new and happening for the first time, as though I suddenly knew why I had been born.'

She said quietly, 'So did I.'

Although his fingers tightened around hers, he still didn't kiss her. 'I knew I couldn't touch Gastano legally. I probably could have arranged his assassination, but that would have made me as bad as he was.'

'No,' she said jerkily.

He shrugged. 'I felt so. Also, it would have left his organisation ripe for being taken over by someone as evil as he was. But I wanted him to pay for what he did—and I wanted to make sure no more innocents would suffer degradation at his hands. To do that, I had to get him to Moraze. I didn't realise you were coming too, or that he intended to marry you.'

Lexie nodded, and scanned his beloved face. 'So you lured him there.'

'But then I decided to keep you out of circulation, hoping that would infuriate him enough to make him show his hand.' He gave a grim smile. 'Well, that was what I told myself. The real reason was because I couldn't bear the thought of him talking to you, kissing you, making love to you. So I organised that accident.'

She lifted her brows, trying to hide the warmth of joy his words caused. 'You're a devious man.'

Rafiq's voice hardened. 'But even though I knew he would turn feral when he realised things were going down, I didn't expect him to steal the helicopter and force the pilot at gunpoint to fly to the castle.'

'I see,' she said, nodding, then frowned. 'What happened to the pilot?'

'He was shot.'

Lexie flinched, and he finished with lethal determination, 'That was why I told my men to shoot to kill.'

'Yes,' she said sombrely. 'When you said that his death was too quick and clean, I agreed, but I understand even better why you felt that way.'

'I'm glad,' he said quietly. 'Now, as I have told you everything, will you please marry me and make me happy?'

Horrified, Lexie felt tears glaze her eyes. 'I wish I could, but I have something to tell you. It's about my father—you don't know who he was.'

'Of course I do,' he said coolly, his frown easing.

She met his eyes, green and steady and direct, then gave a pale imitation of a smile. 'Yes, of course you do. But have you thought things through? If we marry everyone on Moraze will discover that my father was a monster. You didn't want Hani's reputation sullied.'

'Let them say what they want to say. It will not affect us,' he said with the magnificent self-assurance that came from centuries of autocratic rule. In a voice that quietened all her fears, he said, 'I don't care about anyone who will judge you for what your father did—I care only about you. If you will marry me, Lexie, I will love and cherish you all our life together until I die. Neither of us can change our past, but together we can forge a future that will put the memories where they belong—behind us.'

Heart swelling with joy, she smiled at him. 'Then let's do that.'

It took all of Rafiq's iron discipline to control himself. 'I want you to learn to love Moraze as I do,' he said. 'All you have known of it has been a kind of imprisonment—but at home now the flame trees are flowering, and the air is languid and heavy with promise, and there are glories you have never seen waiting for you.'

'I'll love anywhere you are,' she said, the words a vow.

His expression softened. 'And you will be happy,' he said in a deep, harsh voice she'd never heard before. 'I swear it.'

She lifted a misty gaze to him. 'So will you,' she said, not holding back the tears as at last he took her into his arms.

'All right,' Princess Jacoba Considine said, frowning. 'Twirl.'

Obediently Lexie twirled, the silk of her creamy-gold dress swirling around her in a gentle sussuration.

Jacoba inspected her with the unsparing scrutiny of a woman famed the world over for her fashion sense. 'You look utterly, astoundingly gorgeous. Rafiq is going to faint when he sees you.'

To giggles from the two maids who had helped her into her wedding dress, Lexie said with a grin, 'He's not into fainting. I'll settle for him being gobsmacked.'

The maids giggled again, and Jacoba glanced at the clock. 'OK, time to get this show on the road,' she said cheerfully. 'We have exactly three hours before my son announces his desire for his next sustenance.' She examined the Considine tiara. 'I believe that thing weighs half a tonne, but it's worth it.'

'Anything is worth it for Rafiq,' Lexie said quietly, and went out of the room to where Prince Marco, her brother-in-law and distant cousin, waited to escort her to her marriage ceremony.

Much later, in a pavilion overlooking a lagoon scattered with stars, she looked at her husband.

'Come here,' he commanded, holding out his hand as his eyes narrowed in the intent, penetrating gaze that always set her pulse drumming. 'Have I told you how wonderful you looked today as you walked up towards me in the cathedral?'

She smiled shakily, heated anticipation building inside her. Since her arrival in Moraze they hadn't made love, and the time spent away from each other had sharpened her hunger into something close to desperation.

'Not until now,' she said, walking to him over a floor strewn with the petals of tropical flowers. Their scent hung like a blessing in the warm, smooth air.

She cupped his face in her hands, saw the answering glint of passion in his eyes, and knew with rock-solid certainty that this was the start of a long and happy life together.

'I love you,' she said, resting her forehead on his chest, inhaling his beloved scent, taking simple comfort from his formidable strength and presence.

'As I do you. With everything I am, everything I have, for eternity.'

He spoke the words like a vow; to her they were more precious than the magnificent fire-diamond jewellery he'd given her, more precious than anything else in her life.

Then Rafiq kissed her, and all thought of jewels vanished in the magical potency of that kiss, and the glorious promise of their future together in Moraze.

'East of Zanzibar,' she murmured when she could talk again. 'When you told me Moraze got its name because it means east, I thought anything could happen east of Zanzibar—even something so wildly romantic as finding a soul mate. I didn't really expect it to happen, though.'

He leant his cheek on the top of her head. 'But it did. To both of us,' he said in a voice dark with satisfaction, and together they walked hand in hand towards a future as bright and glittering as the fabled fire-diamonds of Lexie's new country, the country that held her heart.

* * * * *

*Turn the page for an exclusive extract
from Harlequin Presents®
THE PRINCE'S CAPTIVE WIFE
by
Marion Lennox*

Bedded and wedded—by blackmail!

Nine years ago Prince Andreas Karedes left
Australia to inherit his royal duties, but unbeknownst
to him he left a woman pregnant.

Innocent young Holly tragically lost their baby and
remained on her parents' farm to be near her tiny son's
final resting place, wishing Andreas would return!

A royal scandal is about to break: a dirt-digging jour-
nalist has discovered Holly's secret, so Andreas forces
his childhood sweetheart to come and face him!
Passion runs high as Andreas issues an ultimatum: to
avoid scandal, Holly must become his royal bride!

"She was only seventeen?"

"We're talking ten years ago. I was barely out of my teens myself."

"Does that make a difference?" The uncrowned king of Aristo stared across his massive desk at his younger brother, his aquiline face dark with fury. "Have we not had enough scandal?"

"Not of my making." Prince Andreas Christos Karedes, third in line to the Crown of Aristo, stood his ground against his older brother with the disdain he always used in this family of testosterone-driven males. His father and brothers might be acknowledged womanizers, but Andreas made sure his affairs were discreet.

"Until now," Sebastian said. "Not counting your singularly spectacular divorce, which had a massive impact. But this is worse. You will have to sort it before it explodes over all of us."

"How the hell can I sort it?"

"Get rid of her."

"You're not saying…"

"Kill her?" Sebastian smiled up at his younger brother,

obviously rejecting the idea—though a tinge of regret in his voice said the option wasn't altogether unattractive.

And Andreas even sympathized. Since their father's death, all three brothers had been dragged through the mire of the media spotlight, and the political unrest was threatening to destroy them. In their thirties, impossibly handsome, wealthy beyond belief, indulged and feted, the brothers were now facing realities they had no idea what to do with.

"Though if I was our father…" Sebastian added, and Andreas shuddered. Who knew what the old king would have done if he'd discovered Holly's secret? Thank God he'd never found out. Not that King Aegeus could have taken the moral high ground. It was, after all, his father's past actions that had gotten them into this mess.

"You'll make a better king than our father ever was," Andreas said softly. "What filthy dealing made him dispose of the royal diamond?"

"That's my concern," Sebastian said. There could be no royal coronation until the diamond was found—they all knew that—but the way the media was baying for blood there might not be a coronation even then. Without the diamond the rules had changed. If any more scandals broke… "This girl…"

"Holly."

"You remember her?"

"Of course I remember her."

"Then she'll be easy to find. We'll buy her off—do whatever it takes, but she mustn't talk to anyone."

"If she wanted to make a scandal she could have done it years ago."

"So it's been simmering in the wings for years. To have

it surface now…" Sebastian rose and fixed Andreas with a look that was almost as deadly as the one used by the old king. "It can't happen, brother. We have to make sure she's not in a position to bring us down."

"I'll contact her."

"You'll go nowhere near her until we're sure of her reaction. Not even a phone call, brother. For all we know her phones are already tapped. I'll have her brought here."

"I can arrange…"

"You stay right out of it until she's on our soil. You're heading the corruption inquiry. With Alex on his honeymoon with Maria—of all the times for him to demand to marry, this must surely be the worst—I need you more than ever. If you leave now and this leaks, we can almost guarantee losing the crown."

"So how do you propose to persuade her to come?"

"Oh, I'll persuade her," Sebastian said grimly. "She's only a slip of a girl. She might be your past, but there's no way she's messing with our future."

* * * * *

Be sure to look for
THE PRINCE'S CAPTIVE WIFE
by Marion Lennox,
available September 2009 from Harlequin Presents®!